Ramón was very, very still. *"Cariña?* You think I'd desert you? Do you think I'm that dishonorable?"

"No." But she couldn't bear him to stay out of pity and a sense of honor. She lifted her chin. "I just don't want you around."

He laughed shortly. "I can disprove that in thirty seconds. All I have to do is carry you up the stairs to your bedroom."

KATE HARDY lives on the outskirts of Norwich, England with her husband, two small children, two lazy spaniels—and too many books to count! She wrote her first book at age six, when her parents gave her a typewriter for her birthday. She had the first of a series of sexy romances published at twenty-five, and swapped a job in marketing communications for freelance health journalism when her son was born so she could spend more time with him. She's wanted to write for Harlequin since she was twelve—and when she was pregnant with her daughter, her husband pointed out that writing Medical Romance novels would be the perfect way to combine her interest in health issues with her love of good stories. It really is the best of both worlds—especially as she gets to meet a new gorgeous hero every time…. Kate is always delighted to hear from readers—drop in to her Web site at www.katehardy.com.

THE SPANISH
CONSULTANT'S BABY

KATE HARDY

MEDITERRANEAN DOCTORS

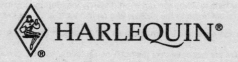

TORONTO • NEW YORK • LONDON
AMSTERDAM • PARIS • SYDNEY • HAMBURG
STOCKHOLM • ATHENS • TOKYO • MILAN • MADRID
PRAGUE • WARSAW • BUDAPEST • AUCKLAND

For Pat—bouncer of ideas *par excellence*

ISBN 0-373-82009-7

THE SPANISH CONSULTANT'S BABY

First North American Publication 2004.

www.eHarlequin.com

Printed in U.S.A.

CHAPTER ONE

'HE'S gorgeous. Absolutely *gorgeous*,' Meg said. 'Tall, dark and handsome—and a smile to die for! When he looks at you, he makes you feel as if you're the only one in the room. And his voice…ooh, it's like melted chocolate.'

Jennifer smiled wryly. Anyone would think Meg was a teenager, not a mum of three and just about to become a grandma for the second time. 'So you liked him, then?' she deadpanned.

'You wait till you meet him, JJ. He'll melt your heart.'

Jennifer doubted that. She'd spent too many years insulating it—and with good reason. The only male who melted her heart was her cat, Spider. And she intended it to stay that way. 'As long as he knows his stuff,' she said. 'We can't afford to carry a lightweight who spends all his time charming the nurses.'

Meg blinked in surprise. 'Wow. Who's rattled your cage this morning?'

'No one,' Jennifer said lightly. 'But you're supposed to be off duty in three minutes and we still need to do the handover.'

'Yeah, of course.' Meg smiled and started going through the list of patients with Jennifer.

Jennifer forced herself to concentrate on the handover, though a part of her mind couldn't help wandering. Panicking. Don't be so silly, Jennifer Jacobs, she told herself sternly. You haven't met Ramón Martínez yet. Meg likes him. He's probably really nice.

And yet she couldn't help it. Even ten years after Andrew, she found herself on the defensive whenever she met someone new—correction, someone new who happened to be *male*. And every time she had to remind herself that not all men were like Andrew, that she knew plenty of nice men. It was a gut reaction that she couldn't quite overcome, despite the counselling she'd had.

'Earth to JJ,' Meg said, waving a file at her.

'Sorry. I was miles away.'

'Dreaming about our hunky Spaniard?'

Jennifer scoffed. 'I've only got your word for it on the hunkiness issue.'

Meg grinned. 'Believe me, any woman under ninety would get palpitations just from looking at him.'

'Better alert the cardiac ward, then.' Jennifer smiled to take the sting from her words and gave Meg her full attention while they finished the handover. 'Right—you have a good couple of days off, Meg. See you on Friday.'

'I will. Oh, and Ramón will be with Stephen Knights,' Meg said, referring to the baby who'd come in for an operation on a cleft palate. 'He should be back from Theatre any minute now.'

'I'll keep an eye out for him,' Jennifer said. Time to move on, she told herself as the other sister left the ward. It's just another day. Another ordinary day. Ramón Martínez is nothing to worry about. And if he is a bulldozer, he's only here for four months. Nothing that bad can happen in four short months.

She was steeling herself, ready to meet him, when Lizzy Bowers pushed past her in the corridor in floods of tears.

Jennifer picked up the couple of files she'd dropped, then followed in Lizzy's wake to the toilets. Lizzy was leaning against the sink, sobbing. Jennifer balanced her files on top of the wastebin and put her arms round the student nurse. 'Hey. It's OK.' Clearly it wasn't—she would have said Lizzy was the least likely of her staff to burst into tears. But it wasn't necessarily something to do with work. She knew Lizzy was going through a rough time at home; maybe she'd had the news she'd been waiting for but praying not to hear. 'What's happened?' Jennifer asked gently.

'Dr Martínez…he was so angry with me. I didn't mean…' Lizzy hiccupped her way through a garbled explanation.

Jennifer squeezed her hand. 'It's just a simple misunderstanding. We'll sort it out.' Though her expression hardened. So much for her thinking she'd been unfair to Ramón Martínez. He'd just bawled out her best student in front of her patient's parents. Whatever Lizzy had done, a public telling-off was completely unprofessional. And it was Jennifer's job, as the senior sister on the paediatric ward, to make him understand that bullies would not be tolerated. Under any circumstances.

'I…' Lizzy was still shaking, still incoherent.

'It's OK. I'll handle it,' Jennifer said quietly. 'Wash your face and take ten minutes out in the restroom. Have a cup of tea then if you're ready to come back on the ward, that's fine.' She gave Lizzy a hug. 'If you need some time off, just let me know and I'll get a bank nurse in.'

'Thanks, JJ.' Lizzy gave her a watery smile. 'I feel so stupid…'

'You're not stupid. You're doing really well. You're a final-year student, you still have things to learn, and you're already worried sick about your aunt.'

'I won't let the team down.'

'I know you won't. And that's what teams are for—to support each other.' Jennifer gave her a wink. 'Go get that cup of tea.' She gathered her files together again and headed for the side room they'd allocated to Stephen Knights.

Standing next to the parents was the most gorgeous man she'd ever seen. Meg's description had hardly done him justice. Ramón Martínez was seven or eight inches taller than her own five feet six, Jennifer guessed. His white coat was a perfect foil to his olive skin and blue-black hair; he had broad shoulders, narrow hips and very long legs. He used his hands a lot when he spoke, she noticed. His eyes were dark and expressive.

But his mouth was the real killer. Generous and full, promising warmth and passion. Meg had been absolutely right about that smile—a smile to die for. For one intensely scary second, Jennifer even found herself wondering what it would be like to be kissed by that mouth. And then she stopped herself. No. She didn't do kisses. She didn't do dates. She didn't do anything of the kind any more. Besides, this man had just reduced one of her staff to tears. He might be gorgeous to look at, but he was also arrogant and in dire need of a lesson in good manners.

'Hello, Mandy. Hello, Paul,' she said, walking into the room. 'Hello, gorgeous.' She ruffled the sleeping baby's hair, then turned to Ramón Martínez. 'Good afternoon, Dr Martínez. I'm Sister Jacobs. I'm sorry I wasn't on duty when you joined us.'

Cool, controlled and terribly English, Ramón thought. And he hadn't been prepared for her in the slightest. She was a completely ordinary woman—average height, average shape, light brown hair cut in an unassuming short style, grey-blue eyes. No make-up, dressed in a dark blue sister's uniform and flat black shoes. She was nothing out of the everyday. So why had his heart rate just speeded up a notch?

Ridiculous, he told himself. He was here at the Bradley Memorial Hospital for a four-month secondment. A relationship of any kind would be short term and pointless. And even if he was prepared to think about it, it couldn't be with someone he worked with. There would be too many difficulties. And then there was Sofía... No, it was all too complicated.

He'd expected the ward's senior sister to be older than Meg—Meg herself had given him that impression—and this woman didn't look much older than her mid-twenties. Clearly she had to be older, or she wouldn't have the experience to do the job.

Automatically, his glance slid to her left hand. There was a slim band of gold on her ring finger. So she was spoken for. He was aware of the stab of regret for an instant before he banished it. 'Good afternoon, Sister.' He shook her proffered hand and lightning coursed through him. Hell. This was a complication he really, really didn't need—especially as it was clearly one-sided. She didn't look as if his touch had remotely affected her. He only hoped that this cool, calm nurse couldn't read minds. If she could, he had a feeling she'd slap his face. Hard.

'How did the operation go?' she asked politely.

'It was a success. I was telling Mr and Mrs Knights about the care their son needs over the next few days.'

He didn't quite understand the look she gave him. Only that she was extremely angry with him—though this was the first time they'd met, so he couldn't have done anything to upset her...could he?

'I've stitched the palate back together in layers. There is one layer in the floor of the nose, then the muscles in the middle of the palate, and then the skin on the roof of the mouth,' he said. 'There are stitches in the roof of his mouth, but you can't see them from the outside.'

'You might see some red fluid coming from his nose and mouth,' Jennifer added, 'but that's very common after an operation like this and nothing to worry about. If you see anything that looks like pus or any real redness around the stitches, that's a different matter, but we'll be checking him every couple of hours to make sure there isn't any sign of infection.'

She might be formal and cool with him, but she had a nice manner with the patient's family, Ramón thought. Reassuring.

'You mustn't let the baby put his hands or anything hard in his mouth,' he added. 'If he keeps trying to scratch his mouth, we will need to use arm restraints to stop him.'

'They look uncomfortable but they really won't hurt him,' Jennifer said. 'But if he scratches his mouth, he might tear the stitches or cause an infection. If we have to use the restraints, he'll probably be a bit grumpy, but just give him lots of cuddles and talk to him to take his mind off them.'

'He shouldn't be in much pain,' Ramón said, 'but if we think he is I can prescribe mild pain relief.'

'What about eating?' Mandy asked.

'He needs small and frequent feeds,' Ramón said. 'He must have enough liquid or he will become dehydrated and develop a temperature.'

'We recommend using a teat with a large cross-cut opening, so you get a steady flow of milk,' Jennifer said. 'Hold him on your lap so he's semi-sitting and feed him slowly— then give him some water to help clean the inside of his mouth.'

'He's teething at the moment,' Paul said. 'He's always chewing his fists.'

'Sorry, but you can't let him. He can't use a teething ring for a while either,' Jennifer told him. 'Though you can rub his gums or use some teething gel.'

'When can we take him home?' Mandy asked.

'In about a week,' Ramón said. 'We will check him over thoroughly before we discharge him. And he will need to see a speech therapist to check if he has velopharyngeal incompetence.'

'It's called VPI for short and it's quite common in children with repaired cleft palates,' Jennifer said. 'All it means is that his soft palate is a bit short or doesn't move enough, so too much air will escape through his nose when he speaks and he'll sound nasal. The speech therapist can do quite a lot to help the condition.'

She was good with parents, and very knowledgeable. No wonder she'd made senior sister at a young age, Ramón thought. But he wished he had some idea why her eyes were looking daggers at him.

'Can we stay with him?' Mandy asked.

'For as long as you like. Did Lizzy give you a card for the coffee-machine?'

Paul shook his head. 'It doesn't matter. We can take turns going down to the canteen.'

'The machine isn't that bad. I'll get someone to bring you a card anyway. You probably remember the routine from the op on his cleft lip two months ago,' Jennifer said, 'but I'll remind you anyway. There's a phone for incoming calls at the end of Red Bay—the number's on the wall above the phone if you need to give it to anyone—and there's a payphone at the entrance to the ward.'

'And don't use a mobile, because it might interfere with the equipment,' Mandy said.

Jennifer grinned. 'Excellent. Well-trained parents. Just what we like to see.'

She was *teasing* them? Teasing the parents of a child he'd just operated on and who were clearly worried about their baby? Ramón was about to step in when he saw that Mandy and Paul were both laughing. The English had a strange sense of humour, he mused.

Though that grin... Lord, if she ever looked like that at him, he'd be a gibbering wreck. The smile turned her face from ordinary to stunning. And he wanted her. Badly.

And then Jennifer was speaking again. 'If you're worried

at all about Stephen or you have any queries, just come and find me or one of the other nurses.'

'Thanks.' Paul smiled at her.

'Do you have any other questions?' Ramón asked.

'Not right now,' Mandy said.

'Then I'll leave you with your son.'

To his surprise, Sister Jacobs followed him. 'I wondered if we could have a quick word in my office, Dr Martínez?'

She was very formal with him, he noticed—and yet she'd used first names with Stephen's parents. The smile had gone, too. Ramón had a feeling he was just about to find out what had upset Sister Jennifer Jacobs. 'Of course,' he said politely, and walked with her to her office.

'Do sit down,' she said, indicating a seat next to her desk and closing the door behind them.

'What's the problem?' he asked.

'You.'

He blinked. 'What?'

'Lizzy Bowers. You bawled her out in front of Stephen's parents and made her cry.'

He gave a short laugh of disbelief. 'She was dropping things everywhere. When I asked her a question, she couldn't answer because she hadn't been listening to what I was saying. And I will not tolerate sloppy nursing, particularly with young children who have just come round from a general anaesthetic and whose parents are worried sick.'

'Lizzy's my best student—she's in her final year, she's passed her exams so far with flying colours and she's very far from sloppy. And I, Dr Martínez, will not tolerate any doctor bullying my staff. You owe her an apology.'

Her voice was quiet and controlled—and absolutely implacable. This was a woman who didn't need to shout to make her point.

But he had a point, too. A good one. He folded his arms.

'Sister Jacobs, perhaps I didn't make myself clear. My patient comes first. And I expect any nurse on this ward to be competent.'

'Lizzy is perfectly competent.'

'Not from what I saw.'

'At the moment she's a little sensitive.' Jennifer bit her lip. 'Look, this isn't common knowledge on the ward, so I trust you will keep what I tell you confidential?'

She'd phrased it as a question but he knew it wasn't a request. He nodded. 'Of course.'

'Her aunt has breast cancer. They're waiting for a biopsy result to see whether it's spread to the lymph nodes.'

'And Lizzy's close to this aunt?' Ramón guessed.

'Her aunt brought her up. So it's more like a mother-daughter bond.'

Ramón nodded. 'I didn't know about her family problems. But my patients must come first. If she can't concentrate on her job, she should take some time off.'

'Keeping busy is the best thing you can do while you're waiting for news.'

'Not when it puts my patients at risk.'

'Lizzy is a perfectly competent nurse,' she repeated. 'If you have an issue with her work, by all means talk to her about it—but in private. Not in front of patients, or their parents, or other staff. I expect my nurses to be treated with respect, as the professionals they are.'

Professional. That was it—the word he'd been looking for. Jennifer Jacobs was professional in the extreme. And he had a sudden wild urge to find out what she was really like. To find out what made her laugh. How her eyes would look in passion—would they turn blue or grey? What did she look like when she'd just been thoroughly kissed?

'Dr Martínez?'

'My name is Ramón.'

* * *

Melted chocolate. Oh, no. Jennifer wished Meg hadn't said that. Because she had the most graphic vision of Ramón feeding her rich, dark chocolate, piece by piece, teasing her by stroking it over her mouth and moving it out of reach so she had to reach up for it. And then he'd reach down to kiss her, and—

No way was she going to call him Ramón. It was too close, too intimate, too… 'Dr Martínez,' she repeated, her mouth dry.

He gave her a quizzical look, and she only hoped he couldn't read her mind. How could she tell him off for unprofessional behaviour when her own thoughts were even less professional?

'Sister Jacobs,' he said softly, 'we've got off to a bad start.'

'Yes.'

'I'll apologise to Nurse Bowers. But I'd like you to have a word with her, explain that if she doesn't feel up to the job then she should take time off so the patients aren't affected.'

'I've already done that.'

'I see.' He folded his arms. 'Then perhaps we can start again. I prefer to work with first names. You're Jennifer, yes?'

She twisted the ring on her finger. Remember Andrew. Remember Andrew. 'Yes.' The word was virtually torn from her. She wanted to stay Sister Jacobs to this man. Aloof, remote, untouchable. Or even JJ, the nickname everyone else in the hospital used. But not Jennifer. It was too personal. Too dangerous.

'And I'm Ramón.' He stood up and gave her a formal bow. 'I trust we shall work well together on my secondment to the Bradley Memorial Hospital.'

'Brad's.'

He frowned. 'Brad's?'

'That's what we call it. The hospital.' Hell. Now she was babbling, and he'd think she was an idiot.

No. It didn't matter what he thought of her. His opinion wasn't important.

'You cared for Stephen Knights the last time he was here?'

She blinked. The question had come out of left field. Or maybe she'd missed whatever he'd said before that. Ramón Martínez had thrown her completely off balance. Frighteningly so, because she'd sworn she'd never let anyone do that to her again. 'Yes. I met his parents soon after Stephen was born. They came to see Dr Keller about the cheiloplasty—' the operation to repair a cleft lip '—and he explained that Stephen also needed the operation to close the cleft palate, to help his speech and to separate the mouth and nasal cavities.'

'And you tease all the parents the same way?'

Now she realised where he was coming from. He hadn't liked the way she'd talked to the Knightses. 'Each patient is different—and so are their parents. I teach my nurses to build relationships with the parents, to help them deal with what's happening to their children. Some like to know every single thing that's happening and to take on as much of the care for the child as they can, some like to joke to take their mind off their worries and some like to know the bare minimum and leave everything to the nurses. Mandy's a joker and Paul likes to know exactly what to expect.'

He nodded gravely. 'Now we understand each other.'

No. She didn't understand him. She didn't *want* to understand him. He was just a doctor, someone she had to work with for a little while. And that was the way he was going to stay.

'I'll apologise to Lizzy, Jennifer.'

'Thank you.' When he continued waiting, in silence, she

knew what he was expecting. She forced the word out. 'Ramón.' It felt almost unbearably intimate, using his first name.

He gave her another of those formal bows and left her office. Still twisting her wedding ring, Jennifer watched him leave. She had to get her overreaction to this man back under control. And fast. Before it landed her in a heap of trouble she really, really didn't need.

Ramón stared into his coffee. Nothing added up about Jennifer Jacobs. He'd watched her covertly on the ward and she'd been the perfect nurse. Efficient, caring, kind. Spending time where it was needed. He'd seen her sitting on the side of a child's bed, soothing away tears, reading stories and chatting while she checked blood pressure and dressings and administered drugs. She never once raised her voice but he'd noticed that everybody always did whatever she asked them, without excuses or delays. She was clearly respected.

But who was she really? She had no family pictures in her office—no husband, no children, no parents, no siblings—and yet she wore a wedding ring. He couldn't work her out. She wasn't even his type—he liked fiery, beautiful Latin women, not quiet, unassuming English mice. And he definitely didn't believe in getting involved with married women. So why couldn't he get her out of her head?

Particularly when he remembered her sitting on the bed of one small child, holding his hand and stroking his hair and chatting to him until the fear had vanished from the little boy's face. He'd seen the little boy hug her in relief, seen the warmth in her smile—a warmth he wanted directed *his* way, too. Yet the minute she became aware of his own presence, a wall seemed to go straight up. Why?

'*Hola*, Ramón. Settling in OK?'

He looked up as Neil Burroughs, the paediatric special

reg, sat down at his table in a quiet corner of the canteen. 'Yes, thanks. But your coffee...' He wrinkled his nose.

'Try the hot chocolate. Though it's a bit sweet.'

'Thanks, but I think I'll pass,' Ramón said dryly.

'So you've met everyone on the ward now?'

Ramón nodded. 'Meg showed me round this morning before I went to Theatre. And then Jennifer took over.'

'Jennifer?' Neil looked blank for a moment. 'Oh, the redoubtable JJ.'

'Why do you call her JJ?'

'Her initials—Jennifer Jacobs.'

Ramón rolled his eyes. 'We do have initials in Spain, *mi amigo*. No, I meant why call her that when her name's Jennifer?'

'We always have.' Neil shrugged. Then he frowned. 'You're not getting any ideas about her, are you?'

'No. I saw the ring. She's married.'

'Widowed,' Neil corrected.

'But...' Ramón stared at him in shock. 'She's so young.'

'She was really young when she was widowed. It happened just before she went into nursing, about ten years back.'

Widowed. Jennifer was a widow. Which meant she was... No. Not free. Which meant he should respect her status. He decided to change the subject—but his mouth had other ideas. 'You called her "redoubtable",' Ramón said.

'Oh, don't get me wrong. She's an excellent nurse, brilliant with the kids and absolutely the best with students— she won't stand for any nonsense but she's got endless patience when it comes to explaining things. She's just a bit...well, remote.' Neil shrugged. 'If someone organises a bit of a do, she always makes an excuse not to go.'

'Maybe she just doesn't like crowds.' Maybe she preferred something more intimate. And Ramón thought he'd better change the subject right now before he disgraced himself.

Neil didn't seem to notice. 'You're probably right. She sometimes goes out to the theatre or the cinema with a couple of the other nurses, but she keeps herself to herself.'

Mourning her husband, perhaps? But according to Neil it had been ten years since his death. And Jennifer was still a young woman. It would be a crime to let her stay buried in work, not living life to the full.

Though he really, really shouldn't get involved. He was only here on secondment. And anyway he had Sofía to think of...

But just before Ramón went to sleep, that night, it was Jennifer's face he saw. And Jennifer he dreamed about.

CHAPTER TWO

RAMÓN tried. He really, really tried to be professional in his dealings with Jennifer. But then he saw her with a small child whose parents had rarely visited. She was sitting in a chair with the child on her lap, reading a story and persuading the child to point out things in the pictures. In her lunch-break, he noted, when she really should have been taking some time out for herself.

She cared about her patients. She cared about her staff. So why didn't she let anyone care about her?

He should walk away. Not get involved. He knew that would be the sensible thing to do. But ten minutes later, after she'd settled the child back in bed, he rapped on her office door and opened it.

She looked up from her desk. 'Yes?'

'May I have a word, please, Jennifer?'

'Everyone calls me JJ.'

Everyone else might, but *he* didn't. He wasn't going to reduce a beautiful name to initials. She was fiddling with her wedding ring again, he noticed. Did she do that all the time, or was it just when he was around? He closed the door behind him and leaned against it. 'Have dinner with me tonight, Jennifer.'

Oh, Lord. She'd heard those words before. Years ago. Then she'd said yes—and it had been the start of the worst mistake of her life. She'd learned her lesson in the hardest way. 'No.'

'Why not?'

Tall, dark, handsome and arrogant—assuming that, of course, she'd want to go out with him. Little mousy

Jennifer, swept off her feet by the first man who'd paid her some attention.

Well, not this time. She didn't make the same mistake twice. She'd learned a lot from her counselling and she wasn't going back to being a victim. 'I don't want to.'

'What's the problem? The time? You're busy tonight?'

'What don't you understand about the word ''no''?' she asked.

'Your mouth is saying no,' he said simply, 'but your eyes are saying something else.'

Damn. He'd noticed. 'I don't know what you're talking about, Dr Martínez,' she lied.

'Ramón,' he corrected.

'Ramón.' It felt as if she were talking through a mouthful of treacle.

'Why do you have such trouble saying my name?'

Her face heated. 'I don't,' she protested.

'You do. And not because my name's Spanish.'

'I'm sure you already have an opinion.'

He smiled. 'I do. I think, Jennifer, that there's something between us. Something you don't want to acknowledge. And that's why you have a problem saying my name.'

'That's ridiculous.'

'Then say it.' To her horror, he actually came to sit on the edge of her desk. Put one hand on her shoulder. Used the other to tilt her chin so she was looking up at him. 'Say it,' he coaxed.

It was the melted chocolate thing again. She'd bet he *knew* he was doing it. He probably did it to a dozen women an hour. She wasn't special to him and she wasn't falling for it. 'Ramón.'

'You're blushing.'

'Because you're annoying me. You're invading my space.'

He folded his hands in his lap. Even though he was no

longer touching her, she could still sense the feel of his skin against hers. Feel the heat of his body. Imagine the warmth of his mouth.

This really couldn't be happening.

'If you were on the other side of the ward and my back was to you, I'd still know the moment you walked into the room,' he said softly.

He said things like that to all the women. Of course he did. He was the sexy Spanish doctor, used to women falling at his feet. And yet what he'd said touched a chord in her. She'd know he was there, too. She was aware of him whenever he set foot on the ward.

'Have dinner with me, Jennifer. Please?'

She shook her head. 'I can't.'

'Can't or won't?'

'Both,' she muttered.

He tipped his head on one side. 'Why?'

She wasn't going to answer that one.

He tried again. 'What's so bad about having dinner with me? Or are all your restaurants as terrible as the hospital cafeteria?'

'I prefer to keep my private life separate from work,' she said.

He nodded. 'I understand. Enjoy your lunch-break, Jennifer.' And then he left, as abruptly as he'd walked into the room.

So he was going to leave her alone? He really wasn't going to bulldoze her?

Her relief was short-lived. Because when she came back from lunch, there was a memo on her desk. A typed memo from the director of Paediatrics, saying that the hospital needed Jennifer, as a senior member of the nursing team, to help look after their seconded consultant. Ramón

Martínez was a guest in their city and they should treat him accordingly.

In other words, she was supposed to show him around and have dinner with him, to make sure he was happy and gave his own hospital in Seville a favourable report on Brad's. If he didn't, the word would spread and Brad's was unlikely to get any more seconded specialists. With the recruitment crisis in the health service, Brad's depended on secondees to fill specialist roles. No specialists meant longer waiting lists, which upset the financial people, who'd say the departments hadn't met their targets and would cut the budget even more. The vicious circle would go on and on and on...

She crumpled the memo with unusual force and hurled it at her wastebasket. The snake! He'd tried one way and it hadn't worked. And now he'd pulled a few strings and manoeuvred things so she'd be forced to go out with him. Well, it wasn't going to work. The next time she saw him, she'd tell him straight.

Except she couldn't. Because the next time she saw Ramón, she was in Stephen Knights's cubicle, writing down the results of his observations, and Ramón had just walked into the room. She could hardly pick a fight with him in front of parents. Instead, she gritted her teeth and carried on with her task.

'Jennifer, may I see you for a moment, please?'

She bit back the 'Go to hell' that had risen to her lips. 'Of course, Dr Martínez.'

This time, he didn't nag her about using his name. He even flushed very slightly. So he must know he was squarely in the wrong, she thought grimly. She followed him into the day room.

'Perhaps we could have coffee for the Harpers and juice for their daughter?'

So now he thought the role of a senior nurse was to fetch

drinks? Her disgust must have been written all over her face, because he added, 'Unless you think tea's better for helping to break bad news.'

'Bad news?'

He nodded. 'Which is why I wish to see you.'

Surely he wasn't going to claim that he needed her to act as an interpreter? Apart from the fact that she couldn't speak Spanish, his English was excellent, with barely a trace of an accent.

'You're good with patients and their families. And I think Mr and Mrs Harper will need a lot of support.'

She frowned. 'What is it?'

Without comment, he passed her a file. She opened it and glanced at the test results on the first page. '"45 XO."'

'Classic Turner's syndrome,' he confirmed.

'Poor kid. Poor parents. Where are they?'

'In the playroom, with their little girl, Charlotte. I'm going to take them to my office. It's quieter there than in the day room.'

And more private. She nodded. 'I'll bring some coffee.'

'Thank you, Jennifer.'

As soon as she walked into his office with the tray of drinks, he gave her a look of relief and introduced her to the Harpers.

'And this must be Charlotte. I brought some juice for you, Charlotte,' Jennifer said. 'Shall we draw some pictures while your mummy and daddy talk to Dr Martínez?' The little girl nodded shyly, and Jennifer handed round the coffees before settling herself on the floor with the little girl, a pile of paper and a box of crayons.

'It's Ed and Fran, isn't it?' Jennifer asked.

'That's right.' Fran had a pinched look about her mouth. 'So, what's wrong with Lottie?'

'It's a chromosome abnormality called Turner's Syndrome,' Ramón said.

'Like Down's, you mean? But why wasn't it picked up when she was born? Or when I was pregnant?' Fran asked.

'Not all antenatal tests screen for Turner's syndrome,' Jennifer said. 'And unless she had a heart condition or showed any signs of puffiness in her hands and feet just after she was born, it's not something that would be picked up until the age of around five or six. There are other signs—such as a short neck which looks webbed because of the folds of skin, low-set ears, short fourth toes and fingers, spoon-shaped soft nails and a low hairline—but unless your GP suspected Turner's, no one would be actively looking for the signs.'

'There isn't any history of it in our family. Well, not in mine,' Ed said, reaching out to take his wife's hand and squeeze it. 'We don't know about Fran's.'

'I was adopted,' Fran said.

Jennifer forced herself to smile. Adoption was common enough. Though Ed didn't have that same look on his face as Andrew had always had when speaking of Jennifer's lack of family.

Then she became aware that Ramón was speaking. 'Turner's syndrome isn't a hereditary disease,' he said. 'It's an accident that happens when a cell divides after conception and a chromosome is lost.'

Ed frowned. 'So what does that mean?'

'There are twenty-three pairs of chromosomes in the human body, and pair twenty-three is the one that decides if you are a girl or a boy. For a girl, chromosome pair twenty-three is XX, and for a boy it's XY. The results of Charlotte's karyotype—that's what we call the chromosome analysis—show that her X chromosome is missing in number forty-five. So, instead of being XX, she's just X.'

'So that's my fault?' Fran asked.

If it had been Jennifer sitting there with Andrew, she wouldn't have asked that question—because he would have made the accusation first. They didn't know her background, so it was all her fault.

'It's nobody's fault. The missing X can come from the father's sperm or the mother's egg. We don't know which.' Ramón spread his hands. 'It happens in one in two thousand girls.'

'What about boys?' Ed asked.

'A boy can't have Turner's syndrome,' Ramón said quietly. 'The Y chromosome can't survive on its own, so the male foetus would be miscarried.'

'But Lottie seems so normal. Just a bit shorter than the other little girls in her class.' Fran sighed. 'I thought the health visitor was making a fuss over nothing.'

'No. With Turner's syndrome, the gene responsible for long bone growth is missing, so without any help Lottie wouldn't grow any taller than one metre forty-three—that's about four foot eight,' Jennifer said.

'So she's always going to be small?' Ed asked.

'She'll always have Turner's syndrome,' Ramón said. 'But we can help with the height. We can give her some growth hormone, starting around her sixth birthday, though it's quite a long course of injections.'

'And then she'll be normal height?' Fran asked hopefully.

'A little shorter, but not as small as if she'd had no treatment at all. Provided the treatment is consistent, of course. If she starts missing injections, it won't work as well. There's also the possibility of using an anabolic steroid to boost her growth.' Ramón shifted in his seat. 'She'll also need oestrogen treatment from around the age of thirteen.'

'Why?' Ed asked.

'Nearly all girls with Turner's syndrome have a problem with their ovaries,' Jennifer said. 'They don't function, so Lottie won't have periods or develop breasts if she doesn't have oestrogen and progesterone treatment.'

Fran shook her head, clearly finding it hard to take in. 'So she can't have children?'

'She may be able to, with IVF treatment,' Ramón said. 'But she needs oestrogen for another reason—without it, her bones won't mineralise properly and she's more likely to have osteoporosis when she's older.'

'There are side effects with oestrogen treatment,' Jennifer added. 'She might get headaches, feel bloated or a bit sick, but that will go away within a couple of weeks.'

'But she's not going to die early or anything?' Ed asked. 'Or be slow at school? Her teacher said she wasn't good at building things, but we thought that was...well, because she was a girl. She's never been into Lego or anything, not like our son.'

'She's not going to die early,' Ramón said. 'Not from Turner's syndrome, at least. Her body doesn't have any oestrogen, though, so she may have memory problems, and she'll find maths and spatial tasks harder.'

'But with support she can do well. There are support groups for families and we can put you in touch with them,' Jennifer said. 'Plus Lottie can come to a clinic here to smooth her path through to adolescence and adulthood.'

'There are some things you need to watch for,' Ramón said. 'Girls with Turner's syndrome have a lot of middle ear infections and that can lead to deafness, so you must take her to the doctor whenever you think she might have an ear infection.'

'Regular hearing checks are a good idea, too,' Jennifer added. 'As well as checking her blood pressure. She's also more likely to get diabetes and thyroid problems, but we can do regular checks at clinic.'

'So where do we start?' Fran asked.

'We can book you into clinic and give you some leaflets about the condition from the support groups,' Jennifer said. 'You need some time to think about it, decide what you want to do and what's best for Lottie.' She gave the little girl a hug. 'Well done, Lottie. Show Mummy what a lovely picture you've drawn.'

'It's me, you, Daddy and Raphie,' Lottie said, handing her mother a piece of paper. 'Our family.'

A tear trickled down Fran's cheek. Jennifer stood up and placed a hand on her shoulder. 'I know it's a bit of a shock, but, honestly, Lottie can lead a perfectly normal life. As long as she's got a family who loves her, she'll be fine.'

A family who loves her. Something Jennifer had never had. She pushed the thought away. She didn't need a family. She had the ward. And that was enough. It had to be.

If he didn't get a move on, he'd miss her. Ramón stuffed his white coat in his locker, grabbed his briefcase and made his way to Jennifer's office. It was empty. Maybe she was changing. He had no idea which way she'd go home—did she live near enough to walk, or did she park in the staff spaces next to the old Victorian entrance to the hospital?— but she would definitely have to go through the reception of the paediatric ward.

He lingered deliberately, pretending to check through some leaflets. And then the back of his neck heated. He turned round to find that his early-warning system was spot on. She was just leaving the ward.

Her out-of-uniform clothing was just as unassuming as he'd expected. A pair of jeans, a loose navy T-shirt and flat shoes. She was a million miles away from the fashion clotheshorses he'd dated in the past. And yet she still had the power to make his heart miss a beat. What was it about her?

As she pushed through the double doors, he fell into step beside her. 'Jennifer, I didn't have a chance to thank you properly for your help with the Harpers.'

She shrugged. 'It's my job.'

'But it was appreciated.'

'Fine,' she said coolly.

'Jennifer, is there a problem?' he asked.

'Only the memo I received this afternoon. I don't like being manipulated, Ramón.'

She'd said his name without prompting this time. That was a good sign…but her eyes said otherwise. She was furious with him. 'I didn't mean to manipulate you.'

'No? So you didn't pull strings to get Pete to write that memo, then?'

He sighed. 'How else was I going to persuade you to go out with me, except to treat it as work?'

'By asking me.'

'I did. You refused.'

'Exactly. And don't use that "I'm a lonely Spaniard in a strange city" line with me. You could have asked anyone else on the ward.'

'True.'

'So why didn't you?'

'Because I wanted you,' he said softly.

'Well, you can't have me.'

'Your blood sugar's low.'

She frowned. 'What?'

'You're grumpy. It's a side-effect of low blood sugar— therefore you clearly need some food. Let me take you to dinner.'

'I've already said no.'

'So you'll leave me stuck in my lonely hotel room?'

Her eyes narrowed. 'You're not staying in a hotel. You've got a hospital flat.'

So she'd been interested enough to find that out. Good. That was a step in the right direction. He shrugged. 'I'm still stuck on my own, in a place I don't know.' She didn't utter a word, but her face said it all for her—she thought he was spinning her a line.

'It isn't a chat-up line,' he said softly. 'I don't know your city. And...I could use a friend.'

She stopped dead. 'Friend?'

'Friend.' He tucked her arm through his and continued walking, careful to match his stride to hers. 'And friends have dinner together, do they not?'

'Ramón, you're bulldozing me.'

'That expression isn't familiar to me.'

She snorted. 'Come off it. Your English is damn near perfect.' His accent was so slight that it was almost undetectable. 'This isn't your first secondment abroad, is it?'

'No,' he admitted.

'So where were you before?'

'Have dinner with me and I'll tell you.'

'You're infuriating.'

'Are you stereotyping me, *cariña*?'

'If you insist on behaving like a stereotype.'

The fire in her eyes was promising. More than promising. He gave her a mischievous smile. 'Maybe I need you to teach me some manners.'

She tried to pull her arm away. 'Leave me alone, Ramón.'

'Have dinner with me,' he coaxed. 'Just as a friend. My treat.'

She was silent for a long, long time. He wasn't sure whether she was going to argue with him or accept he'd outmanoeuvred her. To his relief, finally, she nodded. 'All right. There's a pub by the river. They do reasonable food. Though we'll split the bill,' she warned.

CHAPTER THREE

TWENTY minutes later, they were sitting on the pub's terrace, overlooking the river. Ramón insisted on buying the drinks, so Jennifer accepted a sparkling mineral water. Ramón surprised her by choosing the same.

He looked up from his menu. 'What do you recommend?'

'Aren't you going to order for me?'

He smiled. 'Why would I do that when I don't know your likes and dislikes?'

Andrew had always chosen for her, regardless. At the time, she'd thought it cherishing, that he'd been looking after her. It had only been when it had been much too late that she'd realised that hadn't been his motive at all.

'The salmon's good,' she said. 'It's local—comes from the farm down the road.'

'Hmm. Poached in white wine, with dill. Is that what you're having?'

'Er...yes.'

'Then I'll join you.' He gave her a wicked grin. 'Let me guess. You only ever have two courses—if that.'

She flushed. 'Am I that transparent?'

'You look after others, but you neglect yourself,' he said.

'Whereas you would have three courses, I suppose?'

'Four,' he said, 'if you count the *tapas* before dinner.'

Her flush deepened. 'Sorry. I've obviously brought you to the wrong place.'

'What could be more delightful than a summer evening in England next to the river?' he asked. 'Good food, pleasant surroundings and good company.'

She hadn't exactly been good company so far. She'd been downright surly with him—because she was still annoyed with him for manipulating her into having dinner with him.

'Are we having wine?' he asked.

'Not for me, thanks. I'll be driving home. But don't let that stop you.'

He flicked the wine list. 'No, I think I'll stick to water, too.'

'Nothing Spanish there?' The crack came out before she could bite it back.

He smiled. 'There's nothing wrong with a little patriotic pride. We make good wines in Sevilla. Sherry, of course, plus Manzanilla and Montilla.'

'You're from Seville?' From Andalucia. Andrew's mother's family had come from Castile. So maybe Ramón wasn't another Andrew.

He nodded. 'You know Sevilla?'

'No.' Andrew had never taken her to Spain. He'd fallen out with his late mother's family many years before and the breach had been irreparable. In the early days she'd started learning Spanish in secret to surprise him, please him—but when she'd tried practicing her Spanish on him, he'd just criticized her accent and told her not to speak it in his house again.

His house. Not theirs.

Unlike her cottage, which he'd never set foot in.

Then she became aware that Ramón was talking about his home city.

'Legend has it that Sevilla was founded by Hercules.' He smiled. 'It's a beautiful city. The minaret of La Giralda, the cathedral, the Alcázar palace, the María Luisa park, the Triana bridge over the Guadalquívir, the narrow streets around the church of Santa Ana... And remember, it is the

city of *Carmen*, *Don Juan* and *Figaro*. History, food, art...'
He waved his hands. 'Sevilla has it all.'

He clearly adored his home city. She couldn't help asking, 'So why are you here?' Why hadn't he stayed at home in Seville?

'Because there are work opportunities for me in England that simply aren't there in Spain. And—' He broke off. 'May I order for us now?'

'Fine.'

'What would you like for dessert?'

'I'll pass, thanks.'

When he came back, he gave her a guilty smile. 'I think you're about to be angry with me.'

'Why?'

'There was a specials board by the bar. I ordered us dessert from it. But if you hate it, you're under no obligation to eat it.'

Ordering for her without asking first—just like Andrew. And yet Ramón had offered her a choice. Take it or leave it, as she pleased. There would be no anger, no smouldering sulk that she'd gone against his wishes.

'Am I that scary?'

She blinked. 'I... Uh. No.'

'For a moment you looked terrified.'

'You must be seeing things.' She wasn't going to share those memories. Ever. 'So where were you before you came to Brad's?'

'Sevilla. And before that London for six months. And Manchester and Birmingham before that.'

'All in paediatrics?'

He nodded. 'I like working with *los niños*. Children. What about you?'

'I've always worked at Brad's.'

'No, I mean, why the children's ward?'

Because it was the nearest she'd get to having children

of her own. She forced the thought back. 'I like working with children too,' she said lightly. 'It's very rewarding.'

To her relief, their meal arrived and the subject changed naturally. 'An excellent choice,' Ramón said when he'd tasted the salmon. 'And Jersey Royals. Mmm. I adore these.'

'So you're a foodie?'

'Foodie?' He tipped his head on one side. 'Explain.'

'It means a gourmet. Someone who likes good food.'

He nodded. 'Life's too short not to have the best when you can.'

A quick glance at his wrist told her that he meant it. His watch was a seriously expensive make. Then she noticed that his shirt was silk. And his suit was clearly designer cut. She doubted he could afford them on a doctor's salary—even that of a consultant—so clearly his family had money, too.

So what was he doing out with her?

This wasn't a date, she reminded herself. This was just an extension of work. She was obeying Pete's memo to the letter.

Ramón seemed to sense that she was uneasy because he changed the subject, telling her more about his home city and the children he'd worked with. She'd just started to relax with him when the waiter cleared their plates and brought a small pottery container to the table. He lit a tea-light candle in its centre and Jennifer looked at Ramón. 'What's this?'

'Wait and see.' Mischief lurked in his eyes.

On cue, the waiter placed a bubbling bowl of white chocolate fondue on top of the tea-light, then brought a platter of tiny sponge cakes and strawberries with two forks, which Ramón appropriated immediately.

'This is the nearest they had to chocolate and *churros*.'

'Spanish pudding?' she guessed.

'No, that's *flan*—what you would call *crème caramel*.

Or a dish of sweet oranges. But we had a light meal tonight, so I thought we could get away with this.'

Definitely a killer smile, Jennifer thought. She needed coffee. Or a bucket of iced water thrown over her head. Something—anything—to stop the way her knees were turning to jelly, the way her body reacted to this man.

'Here.' He speared a strawberry on the long fork, dipped it in white chocolate and held it to her lips. 'This is perfection.'

All the tables around them were full. They were in the middle of a very public place. So why did it feel so intimate? Why did it feel as if he was the only other person in the city besides her? And why did she feel that he was offering her something more than the strawberry—something much more personal?

The strawberry was definitely a mistake, Ramón thought, because the moment she bit into it, the sensual awareness in her eyes turned to sheer blind panic.

Why was she so afraid? Of him? But surely she knew he would never hurt her? Regretfully, he relinquished the fork. 'English strawberries have a certain something. It's like eating sunlight, don't you think?'

Gradually, the panic in her eyes receded. Though he noticed that she didn't eat anything else. 'Do you dislike strawberries?' he asked.

'It's not that. They're lovely. I'm just…full.'

In other words, he'd pushed her so hard that she'd lost her appetite. And the guilt in turn made him lose his. He ignored the fondue and the cake and just ate the strawberries. 'Too sweet,' he said in response to her enquiring glance.

'I thought all Spaniards had an incredibly sweet tooth?'

He smiled. 'It's the Moorish influence. I admit that, yes,

I do have a weakness for sticky pastries made with honey. And proper hot chocolate—made the Spanish way.'

She pulled a face. 'Sounds a bit sickly.'

'If you have too much, yes. The trick is knowing when to stop.'

Wise advice—but advice that he couldn't heed. He knew he should stop this now, leave Jennifer be... But he couldn't. He wanted more. Much more. 'Coffee?'

'Not for me, thanks.'

'Then I'll see you back to your car.'

'Ramón, it's very sweet of you, but there's no need. It's perfectly safe.'

'Even so, I'd prefer to see you safely to your car. Humour me? You could always tell me about the buildings on our way back. Teach me about your city.'

She nodded. 'Let's get the bill.'

He was careful to let her pay her way—he knew that if he ignored her feelings now, she'd refuse to come out with him again—and they walked back through the quiet streets to the hospital car park. Jennifer pointed out buildings of note on the way—the church in the market place with stunning stained-glass windows, an art deco shopping arcade, the old toll-house which had once been where the citizens had paid their taxes but was now the tourist information office.

If anyone had asked him what she'd said, he would have just shrugged and said he had no idea. What he'd really noticed had been the way her eyes changed colour, more blue than grey when she was interested in something. The fullness of her lower lip, so promising and so tempting. The way little lines fanned from the corner of her eyes when she smiled. He'd never been so aware of a woman before. He wanted to pull her into his arms, bend her back slightly and kiss her until they were both breathless.

And yet...there had been that panic in her eyes. Jennifer

Jacobs was a challenge. A challenge he wanted to meet. To win. Which meant that he had to take it slowly. Softly. Gently.

When they reached her car, he smiled at her. 'Thank you, Jennifer, for a lovely evening.'

'That's OK. Do you want a lift back to your flat?'

He shook his head. 'It's a five-minute walk at most. The exercise will do me good.' He took her hand and drew it to his mouth. Her eyes widened but he held her gaze—he needed her to know that he wasn't going to hurt her and she was safe with him. Right now, yes, he wanted to kiss her properly. Mouth to mouth. Sliding his fingers into her hair, his tongue against hers, pulling her close against his body so she could feel how much she turned him on. But she wasn't ready for that and he wasn't going to force her. He kissed the tips of her fingers, then folded them down into her palm. 'Goodnight, *cariña*,' he said softly.

Jennifer was shaking when she got into the car. She was still shaking as she drove home. Ramón had barely touched her and yet her whole body had reacted to him, reacted to the promise in his dark, expressive eyes. Reacted to the amber sparks of passion he'd let her see, just for a moment, then damped down again as he'd kissed her fingertips.

It was all show. He probably did this to every woman he came into contact with.

Hell, hell and double hell. She really couldn't let anything happen between them. It would make life too complicated at work. And she didn't want to be a holiday romance, a brief affair. She didn't want for ever either. She'd already done that, worn the T-shirt and paid a heavy penance. She wasn't going to give up her freedom again.

So she'd just have to stay away from him as much as she could.

* * *

Friday was easier, as Meg was back and Jennifer managed to avoid Ramón. She was off over the weekend; and although she half expected that Ramón would track her down to her bolthole, he didn't. She wasn't sure whether she was more relieved or disappointed.

On the Monday morning she was busy dealing with the handover when he came on duty, and he was already examining a new patient when she'd finished, leaving her free to carry out her normal duties without interruption. But although her mind was definitely concentrating on her job, her body wasn't. It was too aware of the handsome Spaniard sitting a few metres away in his office.

'There's some good news, Mr Garrett. The X-ray results are clear,' Ramón said.

'So what's wrong with Tim?'

'It is something called Osgood-Schlatter disease.'

'Disease? It can't be.' Garrett shook his head. 'He only had a knock on the football field. I told him there was nothing broken and he was being a wuss about it.'

Just what he could do without: a pushy parent who wouldn't put the child's needs first. Ramón bit back the scorn he would dearly have loved to express, and gently examined the teenager's leg. 'Is this painful, Tim?'

'Not too bad.'

'Hey. No bravado. On a scale of one to ten, with one being just a little bit and ten being unbearable?'

Tim glanced at his father, then back at Ramón. 'One.'

That glance told Ramón everything. If only there was some way of getting Mr Garrett out of his office, so Tim had the space to tell the truth. He'd just have to do the best he could. What was it Jennifer had said? You had to sum up the parents, find out how they handled things. Garrett was a know-all. So Ramón would blind him with science.

'There's a soft tissue swelling over the tibial tuberosity.

This often happens in young athletes during a period of rapid growth. It's caused by the pull of the quadriceps, which join with the patellar tendons running through the knee into the tibia. When the quadriceps contract, the patellar tendons start to pull away from the shinbone. That causes the pain.'

'I'd prefer that in English,' Garrett said cuttingly.

Ramón just about stopped himself scowling. Don't say the man had something against doctors who weren't English, too? 'All right. You see this bump on his shinbone, just below his knee?'

'It's just a bump.'

'It's inflamed. It hurts when Tim bends or straightens his knee. The muscles in the front of his thigh join to the tendons which connect the muscles to his knee.'

'So he's pulled a tendon.'

'No. It's partly to do with the growth plates in his bones. When he stops growing, the tendons will become stronger and the pain and swelling will go away.'

'So what are you saying? That he can't play football?'

'Not for a while.'

Garrett made a noise of disgust. 'That's impossible. There's a talent scout coming to the club next week. If Tim doesn't play, he'll miss his chance.'

'If he plays, he could end up with permanent damage to his knees. There will be other chances to see this scout.'

'Not like this, there won't! I've worked hard for it and I'm not having it ruined by you. I want a second opinion.'

'By all means you can see Dr Burroughs, but he will tell you exactly the same.'

'In it together, are you? Well, I want to see someone at the top.'

Ramón gave him a wintry smile. 'You already are. I'm the consultant.'

'Then I'll see your boss.'

Just as Ramón was about to ask Garrett what was more important, his son's health or football, there was a rap on the door. 'Dr Martínez? I believe you wanted Tim's radiography results.'

'Thank you, Sister Jacobs. I was just explaining to Mr Garrett that Tim has Osgood-Schlatter disease.' He glanced at the film. 'There's calcification within the patellar tendon and irregular ossification of the proximal tibial tuberosity.'

'Doctors!' Jennifer rolled her eyes. 'If you want a translation, Tim, that means the bump at the top of your shinbone isn't growing properly. But I guess you already knew that.' She looked at his leg. 'How long has it been like that?'

'A month.'

'A week, tops,' Garrett cut in.

Ramón and Jennifer exchanged a glance.

'I'll refer you to an orthopaedic specialist, Tim,' Ramón said. 'For now you need to put ice on your knee for twenty minutes every three to four hours for the next two days. I can give you some anti-inflammatory tablets which will help to deal with the pain. But no sport.'

'When can I play again?' Tim asked, with another glance at his father.

'When you've healed. I'd say in two to four months. No deep knee bending, and if you have any more pain you need to stop what you're doing immediately and rest. Put ice on it, wrap an elastic bandage round it and elevate your leg.'

'If you overstrain it,' Jennifer said, 'your knee will get worse and it will be harder to treat, so it'll get to the point where you won't be able to play again. Ever.' She looked at Garrett. 'So your son wants to be a professional footballer?'

'He's supposed to be playing in front of the talent scout next week.'

'Sorry, Tim. That's rotten luck.' She patted his shoulder. 'But if you rest your leg now, you'll be in a better position to see the talent scout in six months' time.'

'Doesn't anyone around here understand how important next week is?' Garrett demanded.

'Yes. But I'm sure you'll agree—as Tim's coach, I presume?—that his health is more important. Everyone recovers from injury at a different rate, but if he goes back too soon it could lead to permanent damage. So isn't it better to wait for six months and give him a chance than to go for next week and risk Tim not playing up to his usual game and maybe wrecking his knee for good?' Jennifer asked.

'This is ridiculous,' Garrett said. 'I *knew* we should have gone private.'

'A private hospital would have told you exactly the same as Dr Martínez,' Jennifer said. 'Tim needs to wait until his knee's no longer tender before he even thinks about going back onto the football field.'

'As his coach, you can help by making sure he has a proper warm-up routine, especially for his thigh, hamstring and calf muscles,' Ramón said. 'When he can straighten and bend his knee without pain, jog without limping and finally jump without pain, then he can go back into training.'

'I can't *believe* this.' Garrett looked ready to thump something. The wall, a desk—or perhaps the doctor who stood before him.

'Let me take you into my office for a cup of coffee,' Jennifer said with a warm smile. 'It's quieter there and it'll give you time to take it all in while Dr Martínez straps up Tim's leg.'

For a moment Ramón thought Garrett was about to refuse. But then he sighed, nodded and followed Jennifer out of the room.

Without his father's presence, Tim was more truthful about the pain and how long it had been going on. By the time Tim's leg was strapped up, Garrett returned.

'I, um, want to apologise. About earlier. I didn't mean to be rude. I was worried about my boy,' he said gruffly.

'No problem,' Ramón said. 'But you need to stick to the regime until Tim is well again.'

'I know. R-I-C-E,' Garrett said. 'Rest, ice, compression, elevation. I am a qualified trainer, you know.'

Which made it even worse in Ramón's eyes. As a professional, Garrett should know not to push his son's body beyond its limits. But now wasn't the time for censure. 'Good luck. And if you have any worries, come back and see me,' Ramón said. 'The orthopaedics team will be in touch in the next week.'

Once the Garretts had gone, Ramón went in search of Jennifer. 'Thank you,' he said. 'Are you a mind-reader?'

'No. He was pretty loud,' Jennifer said. 'And I thought someone ought to step in to stop you two killing each other.'

'I would never resort to violence,' Ramón said haughtily.

'I was speaking metaphorically.'

'Sorry. I owe you an apology, as well as thanks.'

She shrugged. 'I can handle alpha males.'

'Alpha males?'

'Big and bossy,' she elaborated.

He grinned. 'So what did you do to Garrett?'

'Listened,' she said. 'I had a hunch.'

'And?'

'Sometimes,' Jennifer said, 'people want to live the lives they never had through other people.'

Ramón folded his arms. 'And...?'

'He'd missed out being talent-spotted at Tim's age, so he wanted to make sure that Tim had the chances he never had.'

'Even if Tim doesn't really want to be a professional footballer?'

'Toby just needs time to think about it.'

'Toby?'

'Tim's father.'

Oh. So they were on first-name terms already? Jealousy twisted in Ramón's gut. No way was he letting that bully loose on his Jennifer.

'Anything you wanted in particular? I have some obs to do,' Jennifer said.

'Of course.' He paused. 'But I want to thank you properly. Have lunch with me?'

'Thanks, but there's really no need. I was just doing my job.'

Her voice was quiet but determined. He realised that if he insisted now, he'd lose her. But he wasn't going to give up. He was just going to take a different route. And he knew exactly where to start.

CHAPTER FOUR

THE next morning, Jennifer opened her desk drawer to find a neatly wrapped box sitting on top of her roster sheets. Odd. It wasn't her birthday and any presents from grateful parents were always shared among the ward staff. Frowning, she looked at the card. The bold black script simply said, '*Gracias. R.*'

When she undid the ribbon and removed the paper, she discovered a box of very exclusive chocolates. Her favourites. Ones she never bought herself. The only person who ever bought them for her was Meg, at Christmas and for her birthday.

Why was Ramón buying her chocolates? Or had he done it for all the ward staff? No, surely not—he'd only been with them a week, and she hadn't heard that he was cutting his secondment short.

She got the chance to ask him three hours later, when she was sitting with Sophie, an eight-year-old girl who had had a tonsillectomy, and teaching her how to draw horses.

'*Buenas días, señorita,*' Ramón said with a broad grin. 'And how's my favourite girl today?'

Jennifer stared at him in shock. He couldn't possibly be this blatant! But, no...of course not. He was talking to their patient.

'How are you feeling today, Sophie?'

'My throat's sore,' Sophie croaked. 'And Sister JJ made me eat toast for breakfast.'

'For a good reason, I assure you,' Ramón told her. 'And that's a very good picture you've drawn.'

'Sister JJ's teaching me. Look—she drew a sketch of me, too,' Sophie said, passing the sketchbook to Ramón.

He glanced at the book. 'A woman of hidden talents. I didn't know you could draw so well, Sister Jacobs.'

There had been a time when she'd intended to make her career in art. But that had been a long, long time ago. Another world. In the days BA—Before Andrew. 'Um, it came in handy for my exams.'

As if he sensed how embarrassed she was, he changed the topic. 'Sophie, while I'm here I may as well check your throat, see how you're healing,' he said.

Sophie nodded. 'I just open my mouth and say, "Ah"?'

'That's right.' He smiled, and placed a depressor gently on her tongue so he could shine a light down her throat. 'Good. Very good. I think that calls for jelly and ice cream today, Sister Jacobs.'

'I'll make a note of it.' Jennifer smiled at the girl. 'And I'd better go and see some of my other patients before Dr Martínez tells me off.'

'He won't do that,' Sophie said confidently. 'He's too nice.'

'Why, thank you, *señorita*.' Ramón gave her a formal bow.

Jennifer left the cubicle. 'Dr Martínez, may I have a word, please?'

'It's Ramón,' he reminded her.

She flushed. 'I just wanted to say thank you for the chocolates.'

'Pleasure,' he said. 'You helped me out of a sticky situation yesterday. I wanted to show my appreciation.'

'Anyone else on the ward would have done the same.'

'No. Only you,' he said softly. 'Will you have lunch with me today?'

'No.'

'I know, you don't like being obligated. How about if you buy me lunch, so I'm the one who's obligated?'

'No.'

'Dinner?'

'You don't give up, do you?' Jennifer asked.

He smiled. 'I always get what I want in the end.'

Her eyes narrowed. 'Is that a threat?'

'No, *cariña*, it's a promise,' he said softly.

His words sent a shiver down her spine, and she wasn't sure whether it was one of pleasure or just plain fear. Why couldn't he see that she wanted to be left alone, in her quiet, comfortable life—just her and her cat?

'Why are you wearing those? They look ridiculous with that dress. Don't you know anything? Go and put some proper shoes on—ones with high heels.'

She recognised that look on his face. He'd had a bad day. Someone had answered him back. And he was going to make himself feel better in the way he knew best. Putting her down. She knew all that…but it didn't stop it hurting.

'Come on, come on, we're going to be late! I told you to be ready.'

Ready for another business dinner. Another dinner where she'd know nobody—though if she talked to anyone, he'd want to know exactly what she'd said. What the conversation had been about. Whether she'd shown him up or flirted or…

'Don't you ever listen to a word I say?'

Yes. Of course she did. But where had her attentive lover gone? The man who'd wanted to cherish her when they'd first met, put her on a pedestal. The one who loved music, who enjoyed wandering through art galleries hand in hand with her. The one who'd said he knew he was too old for her and should give her a chance to meet someone her own age who could make her happy, but he loved her too much to let her go. Where had he gone? And just when had this hurtful, critical impostor taken his place?

Keen to avoid a row, she rushed upstairs to change her shoes. And then wished she hadn't a couple of moments later.

'What's this? Sketching?' She felt a familiar churning in her stomach as she heard the paper slap onto the table. 'I hope you're not thinking about going to college or getting a job.'

'I was just sketching, that's all. For me,' she said softly.

'They're not bad. But they're not up to art-school standard. You'd just be wasting your time, trying to get in. I'm only thinking of you, Petal. How hard it would be to face rejection. You wouldn't even get an interview at one of the studios. You're not good enough.' Not good enough. Not good enough...

Jennifer woke with a cry. She sat up straight, drawing her knees up to her chest and wrapping her arms round her legs. She hadn't dreamed of Andrew for months. Hadn't heard his voice criticising everything she did. She'd used the wrong polish on the table. There were smears on the windows. Not enough salt—or too much—in whatever she cooked. He didn't like her friends—they were leading her into bad ways and she was easily led. Not good enough, not good enough, not good enough...

She shuddered. She knew why it was all coming back to her. Ramón. Handsome, Spanish...and determined to have his own way. Just like Andrew had been. Somehow she had to make him back off. She was no longer mousy little Jennifer, scared of being on her own and being found wanting by the world. She'd grown up, changed. She was thirty-two years old, working in a senior position in a career she loved. And she was just fine on her own. Tomorrow she would make Ramón understand.

*   *   *

Though she didn't get the chance. They were both so busy that she barely had time for a lunch-break. And then he caught her in the corridor. 'Jennifer, I know you're busy, but could you spare me five minutes, please?' Clearly her doubts showed on her face because he said, 'It's work. Do you have much experience with cystic fibrosis?'

'Some. How old's the patient?'

'Six months.' He sighed. 'And the parents have taken the news badly. You know better than I do what kind of help is available locally.'

'OK. I'll come now.'

She followed him into his office.

'Mr and Mrs Stewart, this is Jennifer Jacobs, our senior sister in Paediatrics,' Ramón said.

Mrs Stewart had clearly been crying.

'Sister Jacobs, the Stewarts were concerned about little Keiran—he had a big appetite but never seemed to put any weight on,' Ramón explained. 'The health visitor noticed that his height and weight crossed three trend lines on the chart, and he's always had a troublesome cough and slight wheezing. Mrs Stewart had mild asthma as a child and went to her GP to see if that was the problem with Keiran, and the GP sent them here for a sweat test.'

The sweat test, Jennifer knew, was one of the best ways of checking for cystic fibrosis. The child's skin was covered with a chemical called pilocarpine which made him sweat, and the area was covered with gauze and wrapped in plastic for thirty minutes to collect the sweat. Until very recently, babies hadn't been screened at birth. Although now the 'Guthrie test' blood sample collected at a week old was also used for testing for cystic fibrosis, Keiran had clearly slipped through the net.

'Keiran's test showed higher than normal amounts of sodium and chloride in his sweat. And Keiran's stools are large, greasy and very smelly,' Ramón continued.

Again, it was a typical symptom of cystic fibrosis—the pancreas couldn't produce the right enzymes to break down food in digestion, so the child couldn't digest fats.

'So we've diagnosed cystic fibrosis.'

'Which means he's going to die,' Mrs Stewart whispered.

'The earlier we diagnose it, the better chance he has,' Ramón said. 'Every week, around five babies in the UK are born with cystic fibrosis. Thirty years ago, the average life expectancy was around five years—now it's closer to forty years and most sufferers lead relatively normal lives.'

'There isn't any history of it in our family,' Mr Stewart said.

'It's possible to be a carrier without having any symptoms,' Ramón told him.

'One person in twenty-five carries the gene. If both parents are carriers, there's a one in four chance the child will have it, and a one in two chance he'll be a carrier,' Jennifer said. 'Do you have any other children?'

'No. He's our first,' Mrs Stewart said. 'Does that mean if we have other babies, they'll have cystic fibrosis, too?'

'Not necessarily, though the risk is the same as Sister Jacobs said. One in four that a baby will have it, and one in two that the baby will be a carrier.'

'We can arrange for you to talk to a counsellor who specialises in genetic disorders,' Jennifer said gently. 'She can help you decide what you want to do in the future.'

'What does the disease do to him?' Mr Stewart asked.

'Cystic fibrosis is an inherited disorder of the digestive and respiratory system,' Ramón explained. 'His body can't break down food properly, so it doesn't absorb all the nutrients he needs—that's why he isn't growing as much as he should. His body also has a problem with a protein called CFTR, or cystic fibrosis transmembrane conductance regulator, which moves salt and water over his cell membranes. The mucus in his body becomes thick and sticky, and blocks the air passages to his lungs, which is why he wheezes and coughs. He's more likely than the average child to catch a cold or have a fever, and this can turn to pneumonia.'

'So he's going to die,' Mrs Stewart said again.

'If he has no treatment, his lungs will be damaged by chronic infection,' Ramón said. 'But there are a lot of things we can do to help.'

'You'll need to give him some pancreatic enzymes in his food to help break down the starches, proteins and fats in milk and solid food,' Jennifer said. 'He'll also need extra calories so he gains weight and grows properly, plus extra vitamins A, D and E.'

'When you wean him, you must give him a variety of foods and extra calories and protein to compensate for the loss of fat and protein in his stools.'

'Sausages are really good,' Jennifer added.

'If you help him become well nourished, he will cope better with infections,' Ramón said. 'We can give him steroids to reduce the inflammation in his airways and help his breathing.'

'Steroids? Aren't they the things bodybuilders use?' Mrs Stewart asked, clearly horrified.

'No, that's anabolic steroids,' Jennifer said gently. 'These are corticosteroids, which are present naturally in the body, so there's nothing to worry about.'

'We can also give him a nebuliser so he can inhale drugs that relax his muscles and let his airways open—it's very similar to asthma medication,' Ramón said. 'And when he's old enough to crawl and walk and run, you must encourage him to exercise to improve the strength of his lungs. Encourage him to do things that make him get out of breath, such as running and swimming and football.'

'Wheelbarrow racing's brilliant,' Jennifer said. 'He'll enjoy it so it won't feel as if you're making him work hard. It's a stretching exercise, too, as well as helping to drain the secretions from his lungs.'

'I saw something on the telly about someone having a lung transplant,' Mr Stewart said. 'Can Keiran have one?'

'There's a long waiting list,' Ramón said, 'and it's major surgery. There are a lot of risks and I wouldn't recommend it right now. But if he doesn't respond to the drug treatment, we can consider it when he's older.'

'In the meantime, we can teach you how to do chest physiotherapy—it's a kind of vigorous massage that loosens the mucus on his chest,' Jennifer said.

'He'll be prone to infections,' Ramón said, 'so you need to take him to your doctor to get them treated quickly. And vaccinations are important.'

'And that's it? There's no cure?' Mrs Stewart asked.

'At the moment, no, but things are moving. There's research being done into gene therapy and into drugs that can correct the salt and water problem,' Ramón said. 'Things are much better than they were even five years ago.'

'There are some good support groups nationally,' Jennifer said, 'and they have local branches so they can put you in touch with people who've gone through exactly what you're going through now, who can help you.'

'Is he going to be an invalid?' Mr Stewart asked.

'Eighty per cent of people with cystic fibrosis lead relatively normal lives—they go to college, they have jobs, they go out with friends,' Ramón said. 'If you teach him to accept his condition and work to overcome it, he'll do well.' He smiled at them. 'I need to see some other patients now, but you're welcome to stay here for as long as you need. And if you have any questions, I'll be happy to answer them at any time.'

'Thank you, Doctor.' Mrs Stewart shook his hand.

'*De nada*. That is why I am here, to help.'

Jennifer appreciated the way he responded to the parents of their patients. He was caring, warm, kind—but part of her still wondered when he was going to show his true colours, arrogant demands hidden under his pleasant façade.

The next morning, she found out. 'Jennifer. May I have a word?'

'Of course, Dr Martínez.' She followed him into his office.

'It's my day off tomorrow.'

Uh-oh. She didn't like where this was heading.

'And the roster tells me it's yours, too.'

She definitely didn't like where this was heading.

'So, will you join me on a picnic?'

'I'm sorry. I'm busy.'

He made an odd little gesture with his hands—one she remembered Andrew making, too. It turned her spine to ice.

'Maybe we can compromise?'

'Compromise?' she repeated, knowing she sounded stupid but unable to focus properly.

'If I help you with your errands, you'll have time to have lunch with me. The weather report says tomorrow will be fine. We could have a picnic—and you can show me around the area.'

He was spinning his 'lonely stranger' line again. And if she refused, would he tell the director of Paediatrics? Would it cause her problems at work?

'Or if my company's that repellent to you, then I'll go on my own.'

He actually looked hurt. Jennifer felt instantly guilty. He

wasn't Andrew and he did have a point. He was in a strange country, in a place he didn't know, and he'd only just started at the hospital—it was too soon for him to have made friends. And it wasn't as if she was doing anything really important tomorrow. Catching up with the house-work, doing a bit of ironing and weeding… It could wait.

'All right,' she said.

His face tightened. 'Then I apologise.'

'Apologise? Why?' she asked, completely lost.

'That my company is so repellent.'

She shook her head. 'No, that's not what I meant.' Just the opposite—and it worried her. She couldn't afford to get involved with him. 'Of course I'll go with you.'

'I'll help you with your errands first.'

'Thanks, but there's no need.' It was completely irra-tional. If she felt at ease with him enough to spend the day with him, why didn't she want him anywhere near her little cottage?

The Andrew factor, she admitted wryly to herself. Ramón could be dangerous for her peace of mind, so it was safer to keep him at a distance from her bolthole. It would be safer to keep him at a distance, full stop, but work meant that she couldn't. She'd treat tomorrow as if it were work, and it would be fine. 'I'll meet you here at the hospital, at eleven.'

'Thank you, Jennifer.'

And that was it. No triumph, no gloating—just a quiet and simple 'thank you'. Maybe she was misjudging him. Or maybe her judgment was shot to pieces anyway.

Definitely the latter, Jennifer thought the next day when she met him outside the hospital. Ramón was leaning against the wrought-iron railings at the front of the hospi-tal—and she couldn't help catching her breath when she saw him. He was dressed casually enough—jeans, a white T-shirt, a blue checked shirt thrown casually over it to serve as a jacket, and a pair of dark glasses. But he looked utterly gorgeous. In a formal suit or tuxedo, he'd be devastating. And his smile…

No. She'd promised herself she wouldn't get involved. Not in that way.

She just about managed to greet him normally. And then she noticed the picnic basket standing next to him.

Her thoughts must have been written all over her face because he said, 'You're driving. Friends share, yes?'

'Yes.'

'Good. Then this is my contribution—unless you'd prefer to have lunch out somewhere?'

It would be too much like a date! 'No, no, a picnic's fine.'

He gave her another of those smiles that melted her bones, and matched his pace to hers as they walked to her car.

Ramón seemed happy enough to be a passenger—unlike Andrew, who'd discouraged her from learning to drive— and Jennifer found herself relaxing as she drove him out of the city and through some of her favourite parts of the Peak District, telling him about the history of the villages they passed through and local customs.

'I thought we could take a walk through Hollowdale— it's really pretty around here,' she said as she turned into a small car park at the top of the nature trail.

'That sounds good. Shall we have lunch first?' he asked.

'We can picnic beneath the trees,' she suggested.

'Sounds lovely.'

He spread a blanket out on the ground, placed the picnic basket next to it and sprawled out. 'Come and sit with me.'

It was a request, not a command. She could say no. But her body had other ideas and sat obediently beside him.

'So. The green English countryside, the scent of summer flowers, the sounds of running water and birdsong. Perfect,' he said softly. 'Maybe I should have bought an English picnic.' He shrugged. 'But no matter. I wanted to introduce you to *tapas*.'

He unpacked a selection of containers. 'It's said that when the Spanish king Alfonso the Tenth—the one we called Alfonso the Wise—was ill, he had to take small bites of food between meals. When he'd recovered from the disease he ordered that in every inn wine was not to be served unless it was also served with something to eat.'

'And that's how *tapas* began?'

'That's the romantic version,' he said with a grin.

Was it her imagination, or was his accent just that little bit more in evidence?

'*Tapas* comes from the verb *tapar*, meaning "to cover". It started in Sevilla, where we are very practical. A slice of bread was used to cover the glass of wine so no insects could fall into the wine. And then gradually the innkeepers added little bits to the bread. A slice of smoked ham or cheese. Or something a little more elaborate.'

'And you're telling me that you made these this morning?' she asked.

'Ah—no. I bought them,' he confessed. 'There's a little deli not too far from my flat that sells Spanish food. And I wanted you to try the best.'

'So you can't cook?'

He gave her a lazy grin. 'If I have to. But it's what you would call the last resort.' His grin broadened. 'Which is why I won't offer to cook you a meal. I don't think you would enjoy it very much.'

Ramón Martínez could laugh at himself. But that only made him more dangerous...

'So. Is there any food you really don't like?'

'No.'

'Good. Then close your eyes.'

'What?' She must be hearing things!

'Close your eyes,' he repeated. 'If you take one sense away, the others are heightened. You'll enjoy the new tastes more.' Clearly her fears showed on her face, because he added, 'Humour me? As a friend?'

She should say no. This was a really bad move. She knew all that. But she found herself nodding slowly. And then she closed her eyes.

'Open your mouth,' he said softly.

Why did his voice have to be so...so *sexy*? This wasn't fair. She was about to open her eyes when she felt his fingertip touch her eyelid very, very lightly.

'No peeking,' he said.

Yet it wasn't a command. His voice was full of laughter. 'Open your mouth, Jennifer, before I drop this!'

She opened her mouth for the first delicacy.

'It's good,' she said.

'Olives stuffed with almonds. And now this.'

'Ham.'

'*Jamón curado*. This is best Iberian ham.'

He sounded slightly affronted, and she grinned as she imagined his expression. 'It's very nice.'

'"Nice"? Hmm. Try this.'

She was beginning to enjoy this game. 'Cheese. *Spanish* cheese.'

'Of course.' He chuckled. 'It's Manchego. Some people preserve it in little cubes in olive oil.'

Jennifer made a face. 'That sounds a bit...well, greasy to me.'

'Not if you serve it with crackers. And not if you use the finest olive oil.' He paused. 'Hmm. They didn't have the chickpeas and spinach that's famed throughout Sevilla, but they did have this. I think you'll like it.'

The next tiny bite was a riot of flavours. She tried to

distinguish them. 'Prawns and mushrooms, herbs...but I don't recognise what it's served on.'

'Fried aubergine. And the mushrooms are wild.'

She couldn't resist teasing him. 'All that fat's terribly bad for you.'

'Olive oil, Sister Jacobs, is monounsaturated fat. It's very healthy for you. And your body needs fat to metabolise vitamin E.'

She chuckled at the lecture. 'Of course, Dr Martínez.'

He fed her little pieces of toast rubbed with olive oil and garlic, red pepper topped with grilled tuna, and then finally there was a taste she recognised immediately. 'English strawberries!'

'They'd run out of Spanish pastries. And I know you like strawberries.'

She opened her eyes and her pupils dilated with shock. Somehow, during the picnic, she'd ended up lying on the rug too. And now she was looking up at the sky, and Ramón was propped on one elbow above her.

'So you like *tapas*, Jennifer?'

'Yes. They're very nice.' She tried to edge away slightly.

'Jennifer.' He brushed a strand of hair away from her face. 'Why are you so afraid of me?'

'I'm not.'

'You deny it too quickly. Is it me personally?'

'No.'

'A man has hurt you in the past?' he guessed.

'Leave it, Ramón. Please.'

'How can I when...?' He sighed, leaned forward and touched his mouth to hers. Very lightly.

There was no demand, no insistence in his lips. Just gentleness. Questioning. All she had to do was say no—one simple, short little word—and he'd stop. She knew that instinctively.

So why did she end up sliding her hands round his neck?

Why did she tip her head back, offering him her mouth? Why, when he lowered his head for the second time, did she kiss him back?

It was only when she heard a wolf-whistle that she came back to her senses. She and Ramón were kissing—passionately—in the middle of a very public spot. Her face heated and she pushed at him.

To her relief, he didn't ignore her but he moved back and let her sit up. 'What's wrong, Jennifer?'

'We can't do this.'

He raised an eyebrow. 'We just did.'

'No, I mean, we can't...' She stopped, floundering, and glared at him. 'It's not funny!'

'I'm not laughing at you, *cariña*.' He curled his fingers round her own. 'Just at your very English outrage. It was a kiss, that was all. Whoever whistled, they've already gone.' He gave another of those Spanish gestures. 'If you meet again, you won't recognise each other.'

'That's not the point. Ramón, I work with you. I'm your colleague—not your holiday romance.'

His eyes grew almost amber with seriousness. 'I'm not looking for a holiday romance, Jennifer.'

A seriously nasty thought occurred to her. 'Or for ever.' She wasn't going to put herself in that position again. 'I like my life just as it is, Ramón.'

He muttered something and she sighed. 'I don't speak Spanish.'

'You're telling me to back off,' he said quietly.

'Yes.'

'This morning we were friends.'

That had been before he'd kissed her and she'd realised just how dangerous he could be.

She had a nasty feeling she'd spoken aloud when he added, 'I would hate one little kiss to ruin that.'

One little kiss? It had been rather more than that! She

had no idea how long they'd been kissing. But his hair was dishevelled and his mouth was slightly swollen, and no doubt she looked an even worse sight.

'Forgive me?'

Spanish charm. A little-boy smile and a penitent look through unfairly long and thick eyelashes. She didn't stand a chance against it. Even as her head was framing the word 'no' her mouth was saying, 'Yes.'

'I'll behave impeccably,' he promised. Though his eyes were definitely saying something different.

He packed away the remains of their picnic, then smiled at her again. 'I'll put this in the car. And then shall we go for our walk?'

She must need her head examined, but... 'OK.'

He was as good as his word. No pressure, perfect behaviour—he didn't even try to take her hand as they walked together. Part of Jennifer was disappointed, but the sensible part of her knew she was doing the right thing. She couldn't get involved with Ramón Martínez. And there was no point in starting something she couldn't finish.

CHAPTER FIVE

RAMÓN stuck to his 'impeccable behaviour' promise over the next few days. He spent a lot of time with Jennifer—but it was for work purposes only. She was the senior sister, so naturally he'd want to discuss patients with her or ask questions about the way the ward ran. And as for the habit they'd fallen into of having coffee together, with Ramón sneaking in Spanish pastries from the deli near his flat, that was on a colleagues-only basis.

Jennifer had relaxed so much with him that when he stopped her in the corridor and asked for a quick word in his office, she went willingly.

He closed the door behind himself and leaned against it. And that was when her alarm bells started ringing. 'What is it?' she asked.

'Tonight,' he said. 'Are you busy?'

She knew it was a rhetorical question. He wouldn't have asked her without checking the duty roster first and knowing that she wouldn't be working. 'Why?'

'Because,' he said, 'there's a concert I'd like to go to this evening. And I wondered whether you'd like to come with me.'

'What sort of music?' Nope. Absolutely the wrong words. She was supposed to say that she didn't like music. Or she was washing her hair. Or cleaning out the kitchen cupboards… Any old excuse.

'Chamber music. Vivaldi, Bach, that sort of thing.'

'No Spanish composer?' she teased.

He grinned. 'There's only one way to find out. Come with me.'

She'd loved going to concerts with Andrew in the days before they'd married. In the days before she'd realised...

'Jennifer? Is something wrong?'

She forced herself to stay calm. It was in the past, and Ramón wasn't Andrew. If she refused Ramón's offer, Andrew would still be winning. She lifted her head. 'No. Nothing's wrong.' Nothing she wanted to talk about.

'Then you'll come with me?'

'Yes. As friends,' she emphasised.

'Of course. Shall I pick you up?'

She shook her head. 'I'll meet you there.' Then she became aware of the amusement on his face. 'What?'

'Your home. I was wondering what the big mystery was.'

She frowned. 'I don't follow.'

'Every time I suggest picking you up, you refuse. You don't want me to see your house, do you?'

She flushed. 'I, um...'

He smiled. 'I won't push you, Jennifer. We are friends. So you have no need to be ashamed of your house.'

'I'm not.' She lifted her chin. 'I'd just prefer to be independent when it comes to transport.'

He spread his hands. 'I'm not arguing with you, *cariña*. If you prefer, I'll meet you in the foyer. Though I insist that you allow me to walk you back to your car afterwards.'

'All right.' She paused. 'What do you want me to wear?'

He shrugged. 'Whatever you like. I wouldn't presume to tell my friends what to wear.'

Andrew hadn't either—not until she'd married him. She shook herself. She wasn't going to marry Ramón. And Andrew no longer controlled her life. 'Where and what time?'

'The Corn Hall, seven o'clock.'

She wasn't sure whether to be more relieved or disappointed when he didn't suggest dinner as well. 'I'd better get back to the ward.'

'I'll see you later, then. *Hasta luego, cariña.*'

She wasn't sure what shot her concentration to pieces—that gorgeous voice, speaking Spanish to her, or his mouth. A mouth that had only recently kissed her…

Stop it. Just concentrate on work, she told herself. And yet she couldn't. All day she was aware of Ramón. The way he smiled. The way he laughed. The way all eyes were on him.

What on earth was she doing, agreeing to go out with him—even though it was just as friends?

Her doubts deepened once she was off duty. It had been a long while since she'd been to a concert. Years. She was so far out of practice it was untrue. Andrew had always insisted that she dress up. She didn't want to look out of place—but if she wore smart casual, would she look scruffy and show Ramón up?

'Chill out,' she told her reflection. Then she smiled wryly. Considering that it was the middle of summer and she was applying eyeshadow for the first time since the ward's Christmas party…who was she trying to kid?

Even though the foyer at the Corn Hall was full, she spotted Ramón straight away. He was standing in a corner, leafing through a programme. And he looked stunning. The dark formal trousers fitted him perfectly, and the deep amber-coloured silk shirt slightly effeminate—simply heightened his dark good looks.

Ramón seemed oblivious to the admiring glances he was attracting from the women in the crowd. And Jennifer had to fight back her initial thought of, Hands off, he's mine. Of course he wasn't. They were just friends. That was all.

'Sorry I'm a bit late. I had trouble finding a parking place,' she said.

'*De nada.* You're here now.' He looked her up and down appreciatively. 'And you look very nice, *cariña.*'

Andrew wouldn't have said that. He'd have said her

shoes weren't right or she needed a different colour lipstick, different jewellery, a different hairstyle… She shook herself. Andrew's in the past, she reminded herself. And he's staying there.

Even so, she was still on edge when Ramón found their seats. And even more on edge when she realised just how close the seats were together—the man on her right had really spread himself out, so she was forced to move closer to Ramón. And sitting with her knee virtually touching his…it was doing strange things to her heartbeat. Things it shouldn't be doing.

You're not going to get involved, she reminded herself fiercely. You're friends. And that's all.

When the music began, she forgot her fears. The quartet played pieces she knew and loved by Haydn, Vivaldi and Bach, as well as some others she hadn't heard before. She'd forgotten the sheer thrill of hearing music played live, and it wasn't until the interval that she realised she was holding Ramón's hand. She had no idea whose hand had reached for whose, or even how long she'd been holding his, and her throat closed in panic.

He smiled wryly. 'You have nothing to fear from me, Jennifer,' he said softly. He lifted the back of her hand to his lips before releasing her hand. The kiss was so light, so fleeting that she almost wondered if she'd imagined it. Except her skin tingled where his mouth had touched her. 'Would you like a drink?'

She shook her head. 'No, thanks. I hate these interval crushes.'

'Then we'll stay here.' He smiled at her, and started talking to her about the music they'd just heard. By the time the bell rang to herald the end of the interval, Jennifer had relaxed completely with him again. And by the time the concert was over and she'd clapped so much that her palms were stinging, she felt so at ease that she didn't tense up again when he slid a hand under her elbow to guide her through the throng to the exit.

'Shall we have dinner?' he asked.

She shook her head. 'Thanks for the offer, but it's a bit late for me.'

'Sorry. In Spain, we eat late. I keep forgetting it's not the same here.'

'No matter. Thank you for tonight, Ramón. I've enjoyed it.'

'It doesn't have to end *just* yet,' he coaxed. 'If not dinner, maybe a drink? Coffee?' He tipped his head on one side. 'Or if you're feeling very brave, I could make you some Spanish chocolate. *Real* Spanish chocolate.'

She'd intended to make some polite excuse, refuse—but her mouth wasn't playing ball. 'That'd be lovely. Thank you.'

He didn't try to force the conversation as they walked to her car—or when she drove them back to the apartment block near the hospital. She parked in the visitors' section of the car park and they took the stairs to his flat in silence.

Jennifer was nervous. *Really* nervous. Whoever had hurt her had done a very thorough job, Ramón thought. It made him want to break the man's nose—and that sent warning bells clanging in the back of his head. He knew that violence solved nothing. And Jennifer wasn't his property. He had no right to want to murder someone on her behalf.

And yet…

He shook himself. He had to gain her trust, and stomping about like a Neanderthal was hardly likely to do that.

'I, um, didn't have a chance to tidy up before I went out tonight,' he said, giving her an apologetic smile. At least that would make her realise that he hadn't been planning to drag her off to his lair…wouldn't it? 'So I apologise in advance for the mess.'

'That's OK.'

Hell. Double hell. She'd gone quiet on him again.

'I'll make us some chocolate,' he said, ushering her through the front door. 'If you need to use the bathroom, it's the last door on the right.' And he definitely wasn't going to mention which room was next to it. He knew she'd bolt if he mentioned the 'b' word. 'The living room's on the left. Please, make yourself at home.'

'Thank you.' Again, that quiet and slightly shy smile. But at least she was still here, he reminded himself. He hadn't frightened her off completely.

She was going to make her excuses and go, Jennifer decided as she washed her hands in Ramón's tiny bathroom. Thank him for a pleasant evening and flee back to safety. Thus determined, she followed the clattering sounds to his kitchen. And stopped.

Ramón was talking to himself. In Spanish, so she didn't understand a word of it. And she couldn't tell from his expression whether he was angry about something, upset or what.

'Is something wrong?'

'Ah! No. Nothing's wrong, *cariña*.'

'You were saying something.'

'Telling myself that I wasn't going to burn the milk. Or put too much cinnamon in.'

He was *nervous*?

She must have spoken aloud, because he gave her a sheepish grin. 'I am not in the habit of, um, asking women back to my flat. Or making hot chocolate for them. But you're my friend, yes? You will forgive the fact that I, um...' He gestured round at the chaos in his kitchen.

She couldn't help it. She burst out laughing.

'It's not funny, *cariña*. If I burn this, you won't tell any-one, will you?'

'What's it worth?' she teased.

He lifted his chin. 'Go and sit down.'

'Yes, oh Master Chef,' she said with a grin.

Ramón's living room was almost as untidy as his kitchen. She had to move a pile of papers from a chair before she could sit down. The sofa was dominated by a guitar—a classical guitar, obviously Spanish—and the table was stacked with magazines and books. Ramón either didn't spend much time here or wasn't used to clearing up. Maybe his girlfriend did it all for him...

No. Ramón might be Spanish and arrogant—but he was a decent man. He wouldn't possibly ask her out, even as friends, if he had a girlfriend.

'Spanish hot chocolate.' Ramón placed a mug in her hands. 'And the mug was clean, before you ask.'

She believed him. But she also had the distinct impression that Ramón used every single piece of crockery and cutlery in the flat before he was forced to do the washing-up. Gingerly, she took a sip. 'This is lovely,' she said in surprise. 'It's like drinking chocolate sauce.'

'Proper chocolate,' Ramón said. 'The ninety per cent cocoa-solids sort. Melted and mixed with milk, cinnamon and egg yolk.'

Well, that explained the consistency. If it cooled, she'd have to eat it with a spoon!

'And *churros*, of course.' He offered her a plate of pastries.

'Thank you.'

He winked at her, and proceeded to dip a pastry into the chocolate. 'This is the Spanish way of eating *churros*,' he said.

'Right.' She followed suit, and was surprised at how much nicer it tasted. 'I didn't know you played the guitar,' she said, nodding at the instrument.

'Sometimes.'

The words were out before she could bite them back. 'Would you play for me?'

'For you?' He gave her a look she couldn't read, then nodded. 'All right.' He balanced the plate of *churros* on a pile of books, placed his mug of hot chocolate on the floor, then picked up his guitar and sat down in its place. He checked the instrument's tuning, then softly began to play a melody she recognised.

He played well, she realised with shock. Much better than she'd expected from an amateur. Or was it just that Ramón did everything well?

She pushed back the thoughts that came with 'everything'. She was *not* going to remember how he kissed. Or speculate anything of the kind. She seized on the music as a neutral topic. 'I know that. I can't think of the name.'

'"Romance", from *Jeux Interdits*. Though nobody knows the composer.'

'It's lovely. And you play well.'

'Thank you.' He nodded solemnly to acknowledge the compliment. 'Though it's not technically that difficult.' He smiled at her. 'Is there anything in particular you'd like me to play?'

'Something Spanish?'

He immediately launched into something very fast and passionate.

'I don't know that piece,' she said when he'd finished, 'but it made me think of Flamenco dancers stamping to it, their dresses swirling.'

'It's by Isaac Albéniz. *Asturias*,' he explained.

'You play well. Did you ever think about being a musician?'

He grimaced. 'For a time I was torn between music and being a doctor. But I can play the guitar any time to please myself. Medicine was more important.'

'Any regrets?'

He sighed. 'Sometimes. On a bad day. When I lose a patient. That's when I play most—things like the Albéniz, something passionate to express my anger and my sorrow. And then I think of sitting in a Spanish garden among orange trees, listening to a stream running and lying back on the grass to watch shapes in the clouds.' Softly, he began to play a quiet, romantic piece.

It brought tears to Jennifer's eyes. 'That's beautiful.'

'"Romantico", from *Tres Preludes* by Celedonio Romero.' He gave her a sidelong look, and began to play something she recognised. 'It Had To Be You'. Except when Ramón began to sing, it was in Spanish.

Jennifer sat, mesmerised. She'd never expected this in her wildest dreams. Meg would have fainted. The music magnified the melted chocolate effect a thousand times. He could have been singing anything—a shopping list, the entries in a telephone directory—and it would still have sounded incredibly sexy.

He stopped in mid-word. 'What's wrong, *cariña?*'

'Er—nothing.' She flushed, not wanting to admit to what she'd been thinking.

'Have I upset you somehow?'

'No.'

'You sound...discomposed.'

Well, she would. She *felt* discomposed!

'You didn't like the chocolate? You've hardly touched it.'

Without thinking, she said the words that were in her head. 'It's lovely. But I was concentrating on you.'

'On me.'

His eyes went dark. Very dark. And her mouth dried. Oh, no. Why had she said that?

'On me,' he repeated softly. He put the guitar down, and Jennifer's heart started racing.

'On *me*,' he said again, walking towards her. He stood

in front of her chair, regarding her intently, and reached down for her hands. She let him draw her to her feet, and he continued to sing to her in Spanish. She couldn't tear her gaze away from his, and when he finished the song and pulled her into his arms, she went willingly. When he bent his head to hers, she offered him her mouth. And when he picked her up and carried her to his bedroom, she didn't make a single sound of protest. She was too busy kissing him back.

She came to her senses when he set her back down on her feet. Next to his bed.

'I've wanted to do this since the moment I first saw you,' he said softly, drawing her wrist up to his mouth and licking her pulse point. 'And this.' He kissed her inner elbow. 'And I want to do much, much more.'

She realised that he was waiting. This was when she should back away.

'I won't push you into doing anything you don't want to do,' Ramón said, his voice raspy with passion. 'But you should know, Jennifer. It's not a matter of *if*—it's a matter of *when*.'

He sounded so sure. So certain. She glowered at him. 'Because you are irresistible to all women?'

He smiled thinly. 'No. I have a certain amount of charm, but I don't flatter myself that all women will fall at my feet. And I certainly don't expect to take every woman I go out with to my bed.'

Her face flamed. 'Just the naïve ones?'

'You're not naïve. There is something between us, Jennifer. It is…' He lapsed into Spanish. When she glared at him, he shrugged. 'I don't know. I can't think straight. You do something to me, Jennifer. And I think I have the same effect on you. Why fight it?'

'Because we work together. Because I don't want to be your holiday romance. And I don't…' Her voice faded. She couldn't tell him an outright lie. She *did* find him attractive. But it had been a long, long time since she'd made love. She wasn't sure if she remembered what to do. Supposing she disappointed him?

He misread her expression. 'Jennifer. You're not betraying anyone with me. And I'm not betraying anyone with you. It's just you and me. Here. Together.' He touched the pulse that was beating frantically at her neck. 'I can feel how it is with you. And I can assure you it's exactly the same with me. This was meant to be.'

So self-assured. It frightened her.

'I didn't plan to seduce you tonight,' he said softly. 'I planned to enjoy the concert with you, maybe have dinner. If I had planned a seduction, my flat would have been spotless. I wouldn't have taken any chance that might scare you away.'

He meant it.

'I want you, Jennifer. I want to make love with you.' He traced the outline of her face. 'Tonight it's just you and me. Tomorrow we will think about tomorrow. But for now...' He bent his head again and kissed her.

She wasn't sure which of them moved first. Had she unbuttoned his silk shirt, so she could run her fingers through the light sprinkling of hair on his chest? Or had he eased down her zip so he could push her dress down from her shoulders, bare her creamy skin for his mouth?

'*Bonita,*' he breathed, exhaling sharply when he realised that her black lacy bra had matching knickers. He traced the edges with a teasing forefinger. 'Jennifer. So beautiful. *Dame un beso.*'

'In English?' she reminded him.

'Give me a kiss. *Por favor.* Please,' he added. 'Before I go insane.'

She kissed him until she was dizzy. He continued muttering endearments in a mixture of English and Spanish as he undressed her—and when she began to touch him, it was as if she'd lit a fuse. The next thing she knew, she was lying on cool cotton sheets and Ramón was lying beside her, touching her as if he was memorising her body with his fingertips.

'Jennifer. Love me,' he murmured, tipping his head back in invitation.

'But…'

It was as if he could read her mind. He smiled. 'I will protect you. Though you should know that I don't sleep around.'

Even though he could just snap his fingers and any woman he chose would fall at his feet. 'You are prepared?'

'I told you before,' he said huskily. 'I knew this would happen. It was a matter of when, not if. And I wasn't planning to do this with anyone else.' His face softened for a moment. 'How could I, when there is you?'

She stared at him for a long, long moment. And then she leaned forward to kiss him.

He kissed her back, touching her and tasting her until she thought she was going to pass out with need. And then, slowly, he moved to protect her and lifted her to straddle him. *'Quiéreme,'* he said. 'Love me, Jennifer.'

Afterwards, she lay in his arms. 'Ramón, I—'

'Shh. No need to say anything.' He kissed her palm and folded her fingertips over his kiss.

'We've both got work tomorrow,' she reminded him.

'We're both on a late shift. And the night is still young.'

'Ramón—'

He silenced her with a kiss. 'Once is not enough, Jennifer. Nowhere near enough.' He rubbed the tip of his nose against hers. 'And I have no intention of letting you go anywhere. For a little while at least.'

She swallowed. Was he expecting her to stay the night?

'This is our time,' he said softly. 'Forget the hospital. It is just you and me.' He smiled ruefully. 'I think you have made me a little *loco*—a little crazy,' he said. 'Because I've never felt like this before.'

'Neither have I,' she admitted. She hadn't known that making love could be like this.

'Perhaps you shouldn't have told me that,' he informed her. 'Because I'm definitely not going to let you go now.' He began touching her again, stroking and caressing and teasing her towards the peak, and any words of protest went clean out of her head.

Eventually, she disentangled herself from his arms. 'I have to go.'

'Stay with me tonight.'

She shook her head. 'I can't.'

'Can't or won't?'

He'd asked her that before. 'Both.'

He sat up and pulled her back against him, resting his mouth on the curve of her neck. 'Then promise me, *cariña*, that you'll stay with me another night. Tomorrow.'

'It's already tomorrow,' she pointed out.

'Another night, then.'

'Ramón—'

'The only way you are going to leave my bed,' he said softly, 'is if you promise to come back. And soon.' He nibbled her earlobe. 'Very soon.'

She gave a sharp intake of breath. If she stayed here for another second, she wouldn't have the strength to go at all. 'All right.'

'Now I know what it's like to touch you, to kiss you, to love you...*me antoies*. I crave you,' he murmured against her skin.

It was another hour before she finally got dressed. And even then the only way she managed to leave was not to look at him. Naked and smiling, in the middle of his extremely rumpled bed... If she looked at him, she'd stay. And she really, really couldn't do that.

CHAPTER SIX

TOMORROW, we will think about tomorrow.

Jennifer groaned as a soft black paw batted her nose. 'Oh, Spider, can't you let me have two more minutes' sleep?'

The soft miaow sounded exactly like 'no'.

'OK, OK. I'll feed you.' Jennifer crawled out of bed, dragged on her dressing-gown and headed for the kitchen. She switched the kettle on, fed the cat and made herself a very strong cup of coffee before sinking into a chair at the kitchen table. 'Tomorrow' was now today, and she had a lot of thinking to do. Four hours of it, to be precise, before she went on duty and had to face Ramón.

How was she going to face him? Last night...she had no excuses. Not a single drop of alcohol had passed her lips. He'd given her opportunities to say no, to back out...and she'd gone to bed with him willingly. More than willingly. All he'd done had been to sing to her—and she'd fallen straight into his bed.

What now? The way she saw it, there were three alternatives. One: he'd carved another notch into his bedpost and he'd leave her alone in future. Two: he was looking for a fling to divert him while he was on secondment at Brad's, so he'd continue to pursue her—but without demanding commitment. Three: he wasn't looking for a fling—he was serious and he'd pursue her even harder.

She wasn't sure which one scared her most.

She liked her life how it was. Calm, ordered, dedicated to her job, with her spare time spent pottering around the house and her garden, caring for Spider and sketching. She didn't want to go back to the old days, with someone else controlling her life, telling her what to do and say and even think.

But she didn't think that Ramón would take no as an answer. Not now. Not after what they'd shared…

She shivered, dumped the rest of her coffee down the sink and went to take a very long, very cold shower, hoping that the coolness of the water would shock some sense back into her. But by the time she walked onto the ward, she still had no idea what she was going to say to him.

Jennifer just about managed to concentrate on the handover, but every nerve in her body was thrumming, waiting to hear Ramón's voice or feel his presence in the room. Even her favourite student, Lizzy, who'd sobbed with relief on Jennifer's shoulder a few days before at the news that the cancer hadn't spread to her aunt's lymph glands—noticed that Jennifer was distracted.

'What's up, JJ?'

'Nothing,' Jennifer said tightly. She certainly wasn't going to feed the hospital rumour mill. And Ramón had better not either. 'I just didn't sleep well last night.'

'Too humid. Tell me about it,' Lizzy said with a groan. 'It's worse in the nurses' home, believe me.'

Jennifer flushed. She knew all about the limitations of hospital accommodation!

'JJ, are you sure everything's all right?' Lizzy asked curiously.

'Fine. Now, shouldn't you be sorting out some obs?'

'Of course,' Lizzy said, and Jennifer winced inwardly. She never—but never—spoke that harshly to anyone on the ward. If Lizzy mentioned it to anyone else, it wouldn't be long before the whole ward was speculating about what had caused JJ to lose her famed cool!

'*Buenas tardes*, Sister Jacobs.'

And now her early-warning system was letting her down.

Just what she didn't need: Ramón sneaking up on her with no warning. How was she supposed to compose herself when he caught her unawares? 'Hello, Dr Martínez,' she said stiffly.

He frowned. 'Jennifer, I think we need to talk.'

'Not now.'

'Then we'll talk at our afternoon break. My office or the cafeteria—I don't mind which—but we *are* going to talk, Jennifer. Whether you like it or not.' He looked at her, unsmiling, for a moment, and then left her to it.

He didn't need to discuss any patients with her either, so by the time her break came round she was unsettled in the extreme.

'Sister Jacobs. Time for our case conference,' Ramón said, coming to loom beside her.

'Of course, Dr Martínez.'

As soon as they were out of earshot of the ward, he took her arm and spun her round to face him. 'What's the problem?'

'I…' Her mouth was too dry for her to force the words out. How was she going to tell him?

He sighed. 'I know. Last night. I pushed you too far, too fast. *Lo siento.* I'm sorry for that, *cariña.* But I don't regret what happened.'

She flushed. 'I don't think this is the time or the place to discuss this.'

He shrugged. 'So what am I supposed to do? Let you back away, scurry back to your safe hidey-hole and refuse to talk to me? No. I don't regret touching you, Jennifer.' His voice became warm, sensual. 'Kissing you. Tasting you.'

Oh, heavens. She remembered. She remembered only too well and her body swayed towards him instinctively. She pulled herself back with a jerk. She was supposed to be cooling it, not inviting him to take her off to the nearest linen cupboard. 'Well, I do.'

His eyes narrowed. 'That's not how it seemed last night.'

'Last night…was a mistake.'

'No. Our bodies didn't lie, Jennifer.'

So it definitely wasn't going to be option one. Not that she'd ever really thought it would be, deep down. 'I'm not ready for this, Ramón. I don't know if I ever will be—and I just…' How could she explain, without telling him about Andrew? But if she did tell him, she knew she'd see the desire in his eyes turn to pity. And she really, really couldn't bear that. 'Look, we work together. That's the way it has to stay.' For her sanity's sake.

'What are you so afraid of?'

'I've already told you. I don't want to be your holiday romance. And I don't want for ever either.' Which neatly disposed of options two and three.

Liar, her body said. With this man, for ever would be a promise, not a life sentence.

She ignored it. Right now, she wasn't prepared to take the risk. The only person she wanted to control her life was *herself*.

'So you're saying that yesterday was a one-off?'

'Yesterday was yesterday. The past. I would prefer we remain as just colleagues, Dr Martínez.'

'As you wish. And in that case, I imagine that you would prefer *not* to have coffee with me. *Lo comprendo perfectamente.* I understand perfectly.' He gave her a cold bow, turned on his heel and strode away from her. Jennifer watched him walk away, knowing that she had done the right thing—and trying hard to ignore the little voice saying that she'd been brave enough to follow her head but too cowardly to follow her heart.

*　　*　　*

Ramón silently uttered every single curse he knew in Spanish—and English, and French, and the few he'd picked up in Italy. He really shouldn't have pushed her. Hadn't he promised himself he'd take it slowly, gently, let her come to him? And yet, after last night, he hadn't been able to help himself. He'd wanted her desperately. Too desperately—and now he'd frightened her off. Lord knew if he'd ever persuade her to give him another chance. Why, why, why hadn't he been more patient?

Because patience never has been one of your virtues, idiot, he told himself softly.

Colleagues. Just colleagues. The very thought of it sent his spirit plummeting to the soles of his feet. She wanted him to be formal and polite and correct, when all he wanted to do was pull her back into his arms, kiss her, watch the passion flare in her eyes. How the hell was he going to do the 'just colleagues' bit?

For now, he'd just have to stay out of her way.

He managed it for a full hour—and then a new patient came in.

'Hello. You're Oliver, yes?'

'Ollie,' the little boy whispered.

'OK, Ollie. I'm going to have a chat to your mum and dad, and then I will take a look at you, if I may.' He brought out the box of Lego from under his desk. 'Would you like to make me a robot?'

'OK.' But the little boy's eyes were listless, and Ramón noticed that he had trouble fitting the bits together—as if it was too difficult for him to press the pieces on top of each other. And the few words that Oliver had uttered had had a nasal quality about them.

'Mr and Mrs Timms, could you tell me a little about Ollie, please? When did you first notice he wasn't well?'

'He had a tummy bug about a month ago,' Mrs Timms said. 'We'd been swimming—it might have been something in the pool, because I had it too. Crampy stomach pains and diarrhoea.'

'Any blood in the stools?' Ramón asked.

'No. But it was hard to get him to drink anything. The doctor told me to give him ice lollies.'

'It's a good way to get little ones to take fluid,' Ramón agreed. 'How long did it last?'

'Nearly a week, but he seemed to get over it. I sent him back to school, but then—well, he just hasn't been himself.' She bit her lip. 'He's been a bit clumsy, which isn't like him, and he says it hurts to swallow.'

Alarm bells were ringing in Ramón's head. The referral letter had been marked '? GBS'—the GP's short form of saying he thought Ollie might have Guillain-Barré syndrome. The medical history made this more of a possibility. 'And it has been getting worse, this clumsiness?'

'Yes. Over the last week or so,' she said.

'Does he say if it hurts anywhere else?'

'His back,' Mr Timms said.

Worse and worse, Ramón thought. Backache and cramping muscle pains were common symptoms with children who had GBS. 'Is there anything else you would like to tell me about?'

'He's just...not right,' Mrs Timms said. 'I'm sorry, I know that sounds, well, like I'm a fussy mother. But he's not himself.'

'I always listen to parents,' Ramón said. 'You know your child better than anyone else so you're more likely to pick it up when something's wrong. Has he been more tearful lately? Moody?'

'Yes, but I just assumed it was because he was six,' she said with a rueful smile. 'Aren't boys supposed to get this testosterone rush about now?'

Ramón smiled back. 'Yes, I know what you mean. May I examine Ollie now?'

He admired Oliver's robot, helped the boy up onto the couch and examined him gently. As he'd half expected to find, there were no tendon reflexes and there were signs of peripheral neuropathy and weakness. More importantly, the symptoms were on both sides of the body—symmetry was a strong indicator of GBS.

'Can you look to the left for me, Ollie?' he asked. 'And now the right?' The little boy was clearly having difficulty moving his eyes. 'Good boy. And now can you blow into this tube for me, as hard as you can?'

Ollie did so, and Ramón checked the reading. 'And again?' he asked.

The second reading was slightly better.

'And again?'

The third reading was a lot worse. Ramón sighed inwardly. If the tests confirmed his diagnosis, this little boy was in for a rough time. 'Do you like dinosaurs?' he asked.

'Ooh, yes,' Ollie said.

'Would you like to look at my dinosaur book while I talk to your mum and dad again?'

At the little boy's nod, Ramón smiled and gave him the picture encyclopaedia he kept in his desk.

'So what is it, Doctor?' Mrs Timms asked.

'I would like to do some tests to make absolutely sure, but I think that Ollie has something called Guillain-Barré syndrome. It's sometimes called acute inflammatory demyelinating polyradiculoneuropathy, or AIDP, and what that means is that the nerves in his arms and legs have become inflamed and stopped working properly.'

'Is he going to be all right?' Mr Timms asked.

'Most patients recover fully,' Ramón said. 'And because you've brought him in early, we can help him get better much more quickly.'

'But if he's got it, why haven't I?' Mrs Timms asked.

'It isn't contagious. It's a strange disease—you may even

have had a worse tummy upset than he did. We don't really know what causes it,' Ramón explained, 'but we do know that it's an autoimmune condition. It was triggered by the tummy bug and Ollie's body has formed antibodies against the bug. But the antibodies are attacking the wrong thing. They're attacking the outer coat of his nerves—which is called the myelin sheath—and stripping it from the nerve, so the nerve can't conduct messages quickly and the muscles start to become weak. It starts from the feet and spreads upwards, which is why he has been clumsy lately, though it doesn't affect his brain or his spinal cord. Have you noticed anything different about his voice?'

'He just sounds like he has a cold,' Mr Timms said.

Ramón nodded. 'I would like to take some fluid from his spine—it won't hurt him—and do some tests on his nerves. I will also do some blood and urine tests to rule out any other condition, but I think it's likely to be Guillain-Barré.' He sighed. 'The thing about Guillain-Barré is that the weakness will get worse. Eventually Ollie will reach the ''plateau'' stage, which can last anything from a few days to a few weeks, and then he will start to recover. Most children recover in a couple of months, but it can take up to a couple of years.'

'And he'll be all right after that?' Mr Timms asked.

'It depends how long his plateau is,' Ramón said. 'If it's less than two weeks, it's likely he'll make a complete recovery. If it's longer, he may have some weakness afterwards, but physiotherapy will help. But he'll need to be treated in the intensive care unit.'

'Intensive care?' Mrs Timms turned white. 'Oh, no. Oh, Brian.' She grasped her husband's hand. 'Our boy. He's…he's our only child,' she explained to Ramón, biting her lip.

'I know it sounds scary, but ITU really is the best place to help him,' Ramón said gently. 'As the disease progresses, he'll find it hard to breathe and we may need to put him on a ventilator to help him breathe properly. He may not be able to talk, so we need to set up some pictures so Ollie can still ''talk'' to us by pointing at what he wants. He'll be very tired, so we may need to feed him through a tube going down his nose to his stomach—we call it a nasogastric or NG tube—or put him on a drip. He'll also need physiotherapy to make sure his joints stay mobile, and we'll monitor his pulse, how much oxygen is in his blood, his blood pressure and how well he can breathe. The good news is that we can give him immunoglobulins to help with the antibody problem, and this will help speed up his recovery.'

'But he *will* recover?' Mr Timms asked.

'Around eighty-five per cent of patients make a full recovery,' Ramón said. 'He needs lots of encouragement and lots of support, and the nurses and doctors will be there to answer any questions you have.'

'Will you be looking after him?' Mrs Timms asked.

Ramón shook his head. 'I work in Paediatrics, not Intensive Care—but I do know Mitch Brennan, the ITU consultant, and he's very good. He'll look after Ollie. Now, may I do these tests, please?'

'Of course,' Mrs Timms said.

'I'll just get one of the nurses to help me. May I offer you some coffee, tea?'

'Thanks, but we're fine,' Mr Timms said.

'OK. I'll be back in a few moments.'

As soon as he stepped out of his office, he saw Jennifer. 'Sister Jacobs, may I borrow one of your nurses?' he asked.

'They're all with patients at the moment. Is it urgent?'

'I need to do a lumbar puncture, and sooner rather than later. I think the little boy has GBS and I want the test results rushed through.'

She seemed to make a sudden decision. 'I'll do it.'

'Are you sure?'

She gave him a withering look. 'I'm a professional, Dr Martínez. Whatever happens outside the ward, when I'm on duty I do exactly what's needed.'

'That isn't what I meant, Jennifer,' he said softly. 'I know you're an excellent nurse. But with the situation between us…I don't want to cause you any unnecessary distress or embarrassment.'

She flushed. 'I'm sorry.'

'Then thank you for your offer of help.'

Jennifer fetched a sterile kit, then followed him into his office. 'Mr and Mrs Timms, this is Sister Jacobs. She's the senior nurse on the paediatric ward, so you're in good hands,' Ramón said with a smile. 'Now, Ollie, I'd like you to come back on the couch for me. We're going to do a test which will tell us why you're feeling poorly—and it won't hurt you. But you have to promise me you will stay very, very still for me.'

'I will,' the little boy said solemnly.

'Good boy. Now, Mrs Timms, I have an important job for you, too. I'd like you to hold Ollie's hand, to help him stay still.' He'd already worked out that Mrs Timms was happier if she was doing something. And distracting Ollie would help stop her worrying.

'All right.'

'This is called a lumbar puncture,' he said as he moved Ollie's T-shirt out of the way. 'I'm going to put a small needle into the spaces between his vertebrae—the bones of the spine—low down in his back, and collect some of the fluid from it. The lab will test the fluid for me and if the protein levels are higher than they should be, it shows that Ollie has Guillain-Barré.'

'I'm going to put something cold on your back now, Ollie,' Jennifer said. 'You can move if you like, but you need to stay absolutely still when Dr Martínez tells you to.'

'OK,' Ollie whispered.

Jennifer wiped local anaesthetic over the area.

'Time to stay very, very still,' Ramón said, and injected some anaesthetic to make sure the lumbar puncture wouldn't hurt. When he was sure the anaesthetic had taken effect, he took the fluid sample, capped it and handed it to Jennifer, who'd already written out the label.

'I'll take this to the lab now,' she said.

'Thank you, Sister Jacobs.' Ramón helped the little boy back into a sitting position. 'Well done, Ollie. You were very brave.' He went over to his drawer. 'In fact, so brave that you deserve a sticker.' He chose a dinosaur and passed it to Ollie.

'Wow, Mum, look!' Ollie said, still in a near-whisper.

'Do you want me to come back for the EMG?' Jennifer asked.

He shook his head. 'Thank you, but no.'

'What's an EMG?' Mr Timms asked.

'It stands for electromyogram—it's a test to measure the way his nerves are conducting messages and what his muscles are doing. What I'm going to do is put a small needle into the muscle and take recordings of the activity.' He winked at Ollie. 'And our brave boy here won't feel a thing.' He set up the equipment, then sat Ollie in front of it. 'Now, Ollie, can you count how many planets are on my ceiling? And do you know what their names are?'

As the little boy looked up, distracted, Ramón slipped the needle in place. To his relief, Ollie didn't even notice.

Twenty minutes later, he'd finished the tests. 'It looks like GBS,' he confirmed, 'so I'll have a word with Mitch. Perhaps you'd like to go and have a cup of coffee in the restaurant, or maybe Ollie would like to play in the day room while we're waiting.'

Mr Timms nodded. 'But he *is* going to be all right, isn't he?'

'We'll do our best,' Ramón promised. 'The next few weeks will be difficult, but most patients recover without any problems.' When the Timms family had left his office, he sighed and dialled the extension for ITU. 'Mitch? Yes. Yes, I have a case for you. Suspected GBS—I'm waiting for the lab results for the cerebrospinal fluid, but the EMG wasn't good. Yes, his FVC was over 1.5 litres but I think it'll start to dip. OK. I'll see you later.'

He replaced the receiver and sighed again. He could help children get better—diagnose their illnesses, treat them accordingly—but Jennifer was another matter. He wasn't sure what he was going to do, but one thing was definite. He wanted to be more than just her colleague. And, whatever it took, he was going to persuade her to give him a chance.

CHAPTER SEVEN

Two days later, Jennifer was spending her day off in the garden, weeding the borders. Spider was stalking imaginary mice behind the shrubs. She watched the cat playing, half-tempted to stop what she was doing and sketch him. But by the time she'd gone to fetch her charcoal and sketchpad, he'd probably have finished playing and found a comfortable spot in the sun, where he could curl up and snooze for a while.

She smiled and continued twitching weeds out of the earth.

And then she was aware of a shadow falling over her. A large *male* shadow. She shrieked and Spider cowered beside her.

'I didn't mean to startle you,' Ramón said, spreading his hands in apology as she turned round to face him.

She glowered at him. 'What are you doing here?'

'I came to see you,' he said simply. 'You didn't answer your door—then I saw the garden gate was open.'

She got to her feet. 'And since when did you know where I lived?'

He had the grace to look embarrassed. 'I, um, called in a favour.'

'I'll bet you did.' He'd charmed someone in Personnel, no doubt.

He sighed. 'I don't want to fight with you.'

'Then why are you here?'

'I've already told you that. I wanted to see you.'

'There's nothing to say, Ramón.'

'I think there is.' He coughed and brought his hands from

behind his back. 'Though, now I see your garden, these may be a bit pointless.'

He was holding a huge bouquet of red carnations. 'They're the national flower of Spain,' he said. 'I thought you might like them. But this…' He gestured to the flowers spilling over her garden. Deep blue delphiniums, pink foxgloves, light purple buddleia and sweet peas mingled with lavender, Canterbury bells and white philadelphus. Honeysuckle drifted over the fence and there were deep red roses climbing round the back door. 'It's amazing,' he said simply. 'Did you do all this yourself?'

She nodded. 'The previous owner didn't like gardening. He'd left it all to grass.' Patchy grass, at that. So she'd lovingly planned the design, dug out the borders, planted the flowers, reseeded the lawn and tended the plants.

'*Es muy bonita.* Very beautiful,' he said. 'It smells like an English heaven.'

Jennifer blinked. That was what she'd been aiming for— a riot of colour, sweet scents and flowers to attract birds and bees and butterflies. The kind of place where you could drowse the afternoon away. A place where she loved to sit reading, with Spider on her lap, or sketching or painting watercolours, breathing in the scent of summer and listening to the birds.

Spider peeped out from behind her legs, curious to see the stranger.

'*Hola, gatito,*' Ramón said, dropping to a crouch, placing the flowers on the ground and holding out one hand. 'He's yours, I take it?'

'He doesn't—' Jennifer began, about to explain that her cat didn't like men. And then Spider crept across the grass, sniffed Ramón's hand and allowed him to scratch the top of his head.

Jennifer stared in amazement. She'd never, ever known

Spider to go anywhere near a man in the three years she'd had him.

'*Qué pasa, cariña?*' Ramón asked softly. 'What's the matter?'

'Spider doesn't like men. The rescue centre thought he must have been badly treated by one when he was a kitten.'

'Oh, *gatito*. Little cat. *Tranquilo, no pasa nada*. It's all right.' Ramón continued to make a fuss of the cat. 'Not all men are bad. I would never hurt you.'

A lump rose in Jennifer's throat. Was he talking to the cat—or was he talking to her?

Spider shocked her further by actually rubbing against Ramón and then allowing the doctor to pick him up and make a fuss of him. He even rubbed his head against Ramón's chin, as if he'd known and loved Ramón all his life.

'You like cats, I take it?'

He nodded. 'I've always liked animals. My mother has three cats—and they all boss the poor dog about. If he's sunning himself in the garden and they want the spot, they just go and sit on him until he moves. Though nowadays he's so used to it that he just lets them sit on him.'

She could just imagine it—and the picture stored itself in her head for a future sketch.

'Spider. It's an unusual name for a cat,' he remarked.

'Short for Spiderman. Because he's a climber,' Jennifer said. She smiled ruefully. 'Which means when he goes out mousing, he knocks on my window at three in the morning and demands to be let in.'

'You don't have a cat-flap?'

'Oh, yes. He uses it in the daytime, when he's not scrounging milk from the neighbours. But at night he prefers climbing up the trellis.'

Mistake, she thought as Ramón swivelled to look up at

the cottage. Why on earth had she pointed him straight to her bedroom window?

'I see.'

There was a slight smile on his face. A smile which made her feel embarrassed, uncomfortable and yearning all at the same time. 'Why did you want to see me?' she asked.

'Because I can't stop thinking about you, Jennifer.'

'Ramón—'

'I know. You've already told me, you don't want a relationship. I know that you're still mourning your husband.'

She went very still. 'What do you know of my husband?'

'Just that you were widowed tragically young.'

She dug her nails into her palms. 'So you've been asking people about me?'

'No. I simply asked someone to tell me about the staff on the ward when I joined the hospital, and that was what I was told about you.' He shrugged. 'I would never gossip about you.'

'No. Of course you wouldn't. Sorry.'

'Ah, *gatito*. We make life so complicated. How do I tell your mistress that I want to be with her?' he asked the cat. 'How do I make her see that I would never knowingly hurt her, that I would cherish her?'

She'd heard this before. Love, honour and cherish. Admittedly, not in the tiny country church she'd longed for as a teenager, but in an imposing register office, and it had been in front of very few witnesses instead of a large, loving family. Yet Andrew had said the words.

Maybe love, honour and cherish had meant something different to him.

'I've never felt like this before,' Ramón told the cat. 'And I don't know what to do about it. I want to be with her all the time. I know when she walks into a room, even if my back is turned. I smell her perfume when I close my eyes. I remember the softness of her skin against mine, the way her hair falls around her face, the way her eyes go an intense blue when she…' He broke off, smiling wryly. 'Ah, no, *gatito*. I shouldn't speak of such things to you. I will make you blush and you will become a marmalade cat instead of a black cat.'

Jennifer felt a corresponding blush steal over her own cheeks. 'Ramón, I don't want to talk about this.'

'I know. This is why I'm talking to your cat.'

She pulled a face at him.

'Humour me.' His eyes glittered with a light she couldn't quite read. 'Let me tell you how I feel.'

'I don't think this is a good idea.'

'Jennifer, I'm going slowly crazy. I know you want to be left alone. But I just can't help myself. I want to be with you. You're not just a notch on my bedpost. I don't sleep with every woman who makes me look twice.'

Now she knew he was lying. She wasn't the sort of woman who merited second glances. 'I'm just ordinary.'

'Are you, now?' He surveyed her. 'No, *cariña*. You have lovely bones. You will still be beautiful when you have great-grandchildren.'

Her heart twisted. She would never have children, let alone great-grandchildren.

'What did I say?' he asked.

'I don't know what you mean.'

'Your eyes turn grey when you are sad.' He stroked the cat. 'I want to comfort you. But you're like your cat—afraid to be loved. I think you'll scratch me, try to drive me away.'

What could she say? He was too close.

'So I'll just have to learn to wear padded gloves.'

Spider began purring.

'*Gatito*, do me a favour. Tell her that the flowers need to go in water,' Ramón said, 'before they shrivel and die.'

'Are you going to put my cat back on the grass?'

Ramón rubbed the top of Spider's head. 'No. We're quite comfortable, thank you—are we not, *gatito*?'

Spider's purr grew louder.

Jennifer scooped up the flowers. 'Thank you for these. They're lovely.' She buried her face in the blooms. They smelled rich and spicy. Exotic. *Spanish*. Hopefully he'd think the colour on her face was a reflection of his flowers—not that she was blushing because of her memories. 'I'll just…' Her voice faded. There was no way out. If she didn't ask him in for a drink, she'd feel guilty about being rude. But if she let him into her private space… 'Would you like a drink?' she asked.

'Yes, please. If it's not an inconvenience.'

She didn't answer that, just headed for her back door and trusted that he'd follow her. She filled a vase with water and arranged the carnations, then took a bottle of mineral water from the fridge and two glasses from the cupboard. 'It's too hot for coffee,' she said. 'Would you prefer a slice of lemon in this, or elderflower cordial?'

'Whatever you're having,' Ramón said.

She made them both an elderflower cordial and added ice.

He took a sip. 'Thank you. This is…refreshing. Very English. Very summery.'

Her kitchen was too small to sit in, so she had no choice but to lead him into the living room. Spider was still happily curled over Ramón's shoulder. Traitor, she thought, feeling cross and jealous and completely out of sorts. Though at least it meant Ramón wouldn't come too close to her. Which was what she wanted—wasn't it?

'It's a very nice room,' he said, looking round at the pale green walls and cream curtains. 'Cool and very English.' Just like Jennifer herself.

He noted that there were no photographs in the room. Strange: he'd expected to see a picture from her wedding day on the mantelpiece at the very least. Or maybe it was too painful for her, seeing a picture of the man she'd loved so deeply and lost. But there were no pictures of anyone else in her family. Not even one of her cat. And everything was so neat and tidy...the complete opposite to the shambles he lived in. This was like a show home.

Where, he thought, was its heart?

He walked over to the charcoal sketch of a cat mounted on black paper in a clip-frame. 'Did you draw this?'

'Yes,' she muttered.

'A very good likeness—do you not agree, *gatito*?'

Spider purred loudly, and Ramón smiled. 'Even your cat agrees.' He gave her a sidelong look. 'Do you just draw Spider, or do you draw other things too?'

'Other things—but I'm not that good. A professional would have done a much better job.'

She wasn't being modest, Ramón realised. She really didn't think her drawings were any good. Who had crushed her confidence like that? he wondered. Her parents?

'Did your parents persuade you not to be an artist?' he asked.

Her face paled. 'I beg your pardon?'

'You're good—but it takes a lot of luck as well as skill to make a career in art or design. Did your parents persuade you to be sensible instead of following your dreams?'

Her reply shocked him completely. 'I don't have any parents.'

'I'm sorry,' he said awkwardly. 'I didn't realise they had died, too.'

Her face was like a mask. Impenetrable. 'My mother couldn't cope with bringing me up on my own. She abandoned me when I was two.'

Well, that explained why she didn't like people being too close. In case they let her down again. 'You were adopted?' he asked carefully.

She shook her head. 'I was…unsettled at first.' The child from hell, distraught because her mother had gone and she hadn't know why or where or even if her mother was ever going to come back. She'd kicked and hit and bitten and refused to let people close, wanting only the comfort of her mother and not having the words to explain. 'I had foster-parents.' Several sets, according to her records. 'But people only really want to adopt babies. They're not interested in older children.'

Particularly ones with records like hers, even though she'd quietened down again once she'd realised her mother had gone for good. 'If you're small and plain, they don't give you a second glance.' She remembered watching them at the weekends, all the people walking through the children's home, looking for a child to suit them. One who was pretty or good at sports, one who was confident and bright and a pleasure to be with. Not a child who said little and escaped into her drawing. 'So in the end I stayed in the children's home. I suppose that's why working as a nurse suits me—I'm used to institutions.'

Her tone was careless, but Ramón sensed she was trying to hide a deep yearning, a need to know where she belonged. 'Did you ever trace your birth parents?'

'My mother, yes. But she was dead by then and she hadn't filled in my father's name on my birth certificate.' Maybe her father had been married to someone else. Or maybe he just hadn't wanted to stick around. She hadn't had the chance to ask her mother why. There had been no letters waiting for her when she'd turned sixteen, eighteen, twenty-one. No letter at a solicitor's to be passed on after her mother's death. Only the brisk explanation from the children's home: Jennifer's mother simply hadn't been able to cope with bringing up a child on her own.

She shrugged. 'The trail was cold so there didn't seem

any point in digging further, trying to find my grandparents or anyone else who might know who my father was.'

'And your husband? He didn't try to help you find your family?'

'No.'

Her eyes went grey with pain and Ramón could have kicked himself. How could he have been so tactless? Bringing up the subject of her husband, the man she'd loved so deeply. So deeply that no other man could ever have a place in her life… 'I'm sorry, Jennifer. I didn't mean to cause you pain,' he said softly.

'It doesn't matter.'

Oh, yes, it did. And he wasn't going to leave her now—it might be awkward between them, but he wasn't leaving until he saw her smile again. Until her eyes turned blue. 'May I see your other sketches?'

For a moment he thought she was going to refuse. 'Please? I'm not just being polite. I really would like to see your sketches.'

Eventually, she nodded. She went over to the cabinet in the corner of the room and took a portfolio from a drawer. 'Here.'

Ramón carefully put his glass on a coaster on the mantelpiece, then sat down on the sofa with Spider still on his shoulder. There were several sketches of the cat, a couple of watercolours of her garden, studies of a butterfly. 'They're lovely, Jennifer. You have a good eye for a likeness.' He tickled the cat between his ears. 'And you have caught his moods well, too. Playful *gatito*.' He indicated a picture of Spider stalking a bee, then turned over to the next sheet. 'And *gatito* who pretends he wasn't really after the mouse that got away.' Another picture of Spider, this time washing his paw and looking disdainful. 'And…' He flipped over the next sheet and stopped.

It was a charcoal sketch of him from the day they'd spent

walking together. He was lying propped on his left elbow and his right arm was lifted up, shielding his eyes from the sun. His face was relaxed, laughing.

And his expression was that of a man looking at the woman he loved.

He felt as if someone had just punched him. *Love?* He knew what he felt for Jennifer was like nothing he'd ever felt before, but love?

Worse still, if it was written all over his face like that, no wonder she didn't want him near her. Mooning around her like a lovesick puppy, when she was still mourning her husband.

And yet the fact she'd drawn him must mean something.

Jennifer's eyes widened in shock as she saw what Ramón looking at. 'I'm sorry. I didn't realise that was there.' She tried to take the portfolio from him, but he refused to let go.

'You drew me.'

Was he angry, amused, embarrassed? She couldn't tell. But she was squirming inside.

He looked at her for a long, long time. Although his face was expressionless there were distinct amber lights in his eyes. And her pulse began to beat just that little bit faster.

Without a word, he flipped over to the next page. It was another likeness of him, and Jennifer's mouth went dry. It was the picture she'd drawn after they'd made love. A picture of Ramón from the waist up, looking rumpled and sexy, leaning back against a pillow and wearing nothing but a come-hither grin.

'Tell me, *cariña.* Do many people see your sketchbook?'

Oh, no. He really wasn't pleased. 'No. And nobody has seen that one.'

'Good.'

More than 'not pleased'. He was…

Before she could think any more, he put the sketchbook

down, then gently took Spider from his shoulders and put him on the sofa. 'Cover your eyes, *gatito*,' he said softly. Then he turned back to Jennifer. 'I say "good",' he continued, 'because if anybody saw that picture, they would know exactly what had put that look on my face. And they would know who was responsible. The artist herself.' He tipped his head slightly to one side. 'And that, *mi amor*, would ruin your reputation at the hospital. The gossip-mongers would have a field day.'

She stood very, very still.

He took her right hand. Drew her fingers up to his mouth and kissed each fingertip in turn, his gaze never leaving hers. 'You drew me,' he said softly, 'like that. After we'd made love. So it must have meant something to you.'

She couldn't move. Couldn't speak. Panic oozed from every pore.

Gently, he pulled her to him. Kissed the tip of her nose. Her eyelids. 'I know you loved your husband very deeply,' he said softly, 'but it was a long time ago. And you can't live in the past for ever. He'll always have a place in your heart, and any man who loved you would respect that. But now it's time to move on, Jennifer. Open your heart and let yourself find love again.'

She couldn't possibly explain. Right now she couldn't muster her thoughts into any sort of coherence, let alone talk to him. She was too aware of his lips against her skin, making every nerve-end spring to life. Too aware of his clean male scent. Too aware of his hands—one lightly curved on her waist, holding her to him, and the other tracing the outline of her face, stroking her lower lip.

What else could she do but open her mouth? And when he bent his head to kiss her again, she found her hands twining round his neck. Drawing him closer.

'Tell me,' he said as he broke the kiss. 'Tell me this

means something to you.' It was a command—but it was also a plea.

'It does.'

Amber lights sparked in his eyes. This time, when he kissed her, it was more demanding. More passionate. Needy.

'Give me a chance, *cariña*,' he murmured against her ear. 'Let me love you. Let me show you how good it can be.'

She pulled back and his eyes darkened in puzzlement and pain. And then he smiled as she took his hand and led him out of the room. He followed her up the stairs, and she closed her bedroom door behind them.

'*Mi amor*,' he said softly, and kissed her again.

'The curtains,' she said when he broke the kiss.

He shook his head. 'Your bedroom looks over the garden. Nobody can see in. And I don't want to shut out the sun—I want it to light your body, show me your beauty.' As if he could read her mind, before she could protest, he placed a finger on her lips. 'And you are beautiful, Jennifer.'

He caressed every inch of skin as he undressed her. And when they were both naked, he traced the outline of her curves with his palms. 'I wish I had your skill with a pencil,' he said. 'I'd draw you like this.' He led her over to the cheval mirror in the corner of her bedroom, spun her round to face the mirror and drew her back against his body, spreading his fingers across the flat planes of her stomach. 'I'd like to draw *us* like this,' he added huskily.

She could see what he meant. His olive skin and dark hair were a perfect foil to her own paler colouring.

'You once told me you were ordinary,' he said, nuzzling her shoulder. 'I think not. Your hair's like an English cornfield when the sun lights it, your eyes like the sky. Blue like the summer when you are happy, grey like November when you are sad.' He traced her lips with his forefinger. 'Your mouth is a rosebud about to open and blossom.'

She couldn't resist opening her mouth and biting his finger gently.

His eyes turned to molten amber, and he pulled her closer to him, linking his hands round her waist. 'I want you, *querida*. I want you so much it hurts.'

In answer, she reached up to caress his face. In a second he'd spun her round to face him and was kissing her again, kissing her until she'd blocked out the sunlight, blocked out the birdsong, blocked out everything except him.

He lifted her and placed her gently on her bed. The duvet hit the floor and then he was beside her, his weight dipping the mattress, the warmth of his skin in sharp contrast to the coolness of her cotton sheets.

'You and I... This is meant to be,' he said softly.

'But—'

He kissed her words away. 'No buts, Jennifer. Just you and I. Together.' He licked the hollows of her collarbones.

She gave a sharp intake of breath. 'I can't think straight when you do that.'

'Hmm. I don't think you should have told me that.' He grinned and did it again, and she arched back on the bed. He traced the valley between her breasts, then nuzzled his way down her abdomen. She slid her hands into his hair, urging him on.

'Tell me you want me,' he murmured against her skin. 'Tell me you want me as much as I want you.'

'I want you.' The words were virtually ripped from her.

'That's a start,' he said, and she stopped thinking as he touched her, tasted her, took her higher and higher and finally over the edge.

She was still shaking when he shifted to lie beside her and gather her into his arms. 'Ramón...'

'That time was for you.' He was doing the melted-

An Important Message
from the Editors

Dear Reader,

If you'd enjoy reading romance novels with larger print that's easier on your eyes, let us send you *TWO FREE* HARLEQUIN INTRIGUE® NOVELS in our NEW LARGER-PRINT EDITION. These books are complete and unabridged, but the type is set about 25% bigger to make it easier to read. Look inside for an actual-size sample.

By the way, you'll also get a surprise gift with your two free books!

Pam Powers

Peel off Seal and Place Inside...

THE RIGHT WOMAN

she'd thought she was fine. It took Daniel's words and Brooke's question to make her realize she was far from a full recovery.

She'd made a start with her sister's help and she intended to go forward now. Sarah felt as if she'd been living in a darkened room and someone had suddenly opened a door, letting in the fresh air and sunshine. She could feel its warmth slowly seeping into the coldest part of her. The feeling was liberating. She realized it was only a small step and she had a long way to go, but she was ready to face life again with Serena and her family behind her.

All too soon, they were saying goodbye and Sarah experienced a moment of sadness for all years she and Serena had missed. But they each other now, and that's what

NTED IN THE U.S.A.

lisher acknowledges the copyright holder of the excerpt from this individual work as follows:
RIGHT WOMAN Copyright © 2004 by Linda Warren. All rights reserved.
nd TM are trademarks owned and used by the trademark owner and/or its licensee.

YOURS FREE!
*You'll get a great mystery gift with
your two free larger-print books!*

GET TWO FREE LARGER-PRINT BOOKS!

YES! Please send me two free Harlequin Intrigue® romantic suspense novels in the larger-print edition, and my free mystery gift, too. I understand that I am under no obligation to purchase anything, as explained on the back of this insert.

199 HDL D7U7

399 HDL D7U9

FIRST NAME	LAST NAME

ADDRESS

APT.#	CITY

STATE/PROV.	ZIP/POSTAL CODE

Are you a current Harlequin Intrigue® subscriber and want to receive the larger-print edition?
Call 1-800-221-5011 today!

▼ DETACH AND MAIL CARD TODAY! ▼

(H-I-LPP-05/05) © 2004 Harlequin Enterprises Ltd.

The Harlequin Reader Service™ — Here's How It Works:

Accepting your 2 free Harlequin Intrigue® larger-print books and gift places you under no obligation to buy anything. You may keep the books and gift and return the shipping statement marked "cancel." If you do not cancel, about a month later we'll send you 6 additional Harlequin Intrigue larger-print books and bill you just $4.49 each in the U.S., or $5.24 each in Canada, plus 25¢ shipping & handling per book and applicable taxes if any.* That's the complete price and — compared to cover prices of $5.24 each in the U.S. and $6.24 each in Canada — it's quite a bargain! You may cancel at any time, but if you choose to continue, every month we'll send you 6 more books, which you may either purchase at the discount price or return to us and cancel your subscription.

*Terms and prices subject to change without notice. Sales tax applicable in N.Y. Canadian residents will be charged applicable provincial taxes and GST.

If offer card is missing write to: Harlequin Reader Service, 3010 Walden Ave., P.O. Box 1867, Buffalo, NY 14240-1867

BUSINESS REPLY MAIL

FIRST-CLASS MAIL   PERMIT NO. 717-003   BUFFALO, NY

POSTAGE WILL BE PAID BY ADDRESSEE

HARLEQUIN READER SERVICE
3010 WALDEN AVE
PO BOX 1867
BUFFALO NY 14240-9952

NO POSTAGE
NECESSARY
IF MAILED
IN THE
UNITED STATES

chocolate thing with his voice again. 'This is for us.' This time he made love with her slowly, gently. Persuaded her to mirror his actions, match him kiss for kiss, taste for taste, touch for touch. She felt herself splinter round him—and he was there with her, calling her name, saying something in Spanish she didn't understand, and yet she didn't need a translation. She simply knew.

Te deseo con toda mi corazón.

CHAPTER EIGHT

THE next few weeks were the happiest that Jennifer had ever known. Although she and Ramón were careful to be professional with each other on the ward—they'd agreed tacitly not to let the hospital grapevine hear a whisper of what was happening between them—she spent all her free time with him. They even sneaked a couple of lunchtimes together—a snatched hour at his flat, where he fed her choice bits of ham and olives and Spanish cheese and crusty bread, and made love to her with a passion that had a greater edge because his pager could have interrupted them at any second if he had been needed on the ward. And if her hair was still damp from his shower when they returned to the ward, nobody noticed. At least, nobody commented.

Although Jennifer had worried that if she let Ramón into her life, he'd try to take over in the same way that Andrew had, he didn't. He didn't try to change her, didn't buy her clothes or shoes as a way of making her look the way he thought she should look, didn't want her to change her hair or her make-up or her perfume or anything at all. The first night he stayed over, he got up before she did the next morning and made her a mug of coffee just the way she liked it.

'It's the little things that count,' he said simply, when she asked why. 'And I don't expect you to wait on me, *mi amor*.'

Ramón introduced her to all sorts of things she'd never done. He carried her into a photograph booth and sat her on his lap and pulled faces at her in the mirror until she was laughing; he gave her two of the tiny snapshots to keep, and placed the others in his wallet. He left her romantic little notes in all sorts of places—her fridge, her coffee-jar, underneath her pillow. He drew a heart with their initials in the steam on her bathroom mirror. They went out to the Blue John mines and took a boat ride through the flooded caverns, admiring the stalagmites and stalagtites—and he bought her a heart carved out of a piece of blue john as a keepsake.

One night, Ramón danced with her barefoot on her lawn under the stars, singing softly to her in Spanish. 'I want to make love with you,' he murmured.

She nodded and took his hand, as if to lead him indoors.

'No.' He stopped her and kissed her fingers. *'Here.'*

'Here?' She was faintly shocked. He wanted to make love in her garden? Outside?

'Your garden isn't overlooked. No one can see us,' he said softly. 'And I want to love you here, under the stars. Here in your little piece of paradise, among the sounds of the owls and the scent of your flowers.'

'Night-scented stocks,' she said.

'Ah, my Jennifer. Always so precise. It's one of the things I adore about you.' He kissed her.

Adrenalin pumped through her system as he began unbuttoning her shirt. It was the kind of thing she'd never, ever thought of doing before. And yet as he kissed her, as he touched her, she relaxed. Closed her eyes. Let the sounds and scents of the night work their magic on her. And when she came, it was with her eyes wide open, looking up at the stars.

They both knew that his secondment would come to an end, but the subject was never brought up. What would happen next? It didn't matter. As Ramón had said, *Tomorrow we will think about tomorrow*. All that mattered was here and now, being together, making love, storing memories. Good memories, to lay all her bad ones to rest.

The day Ramón posed for her was one of the best. She bossed him about, made him sit still, and he didn't complain once—even when his muscles ached. Andrew had never sat for her. The sketches she'd done of him had all been from memory, done while he'd been out of the house. But Jennifer adored drawing from life. Capturing the exact sheen of Ramón's skin in the light, the play of his muscles under his skin, the creases at the corner of his eyes when he smiled. The sensual curve of his mouth, the love shining from his eyes, his sheer joy for living. She drew all of it in charcoal, in pencil, in pastels.

When she'd finished, she let him see.

'I don't know what to say,' he admitted as he leafed through the pictures.

Her heartbeat quickened. So he thought they were no good, but didn't want to hurt her by saying so?

Her worries must have shown on her face, because he brushed her cheek with the backs of his fingers in a comforting gesture. 'I'm lost for words because you're not good at accepting praise, *mi amor*. And it feels strange to admire myself. But you're good. Very good.' He picked out one particular sketch. 'May I have this, please?'

He actually wanted one of her drawings? 'Yes.'

'They say that a picture is worth a thousand words. And this says everything.' His voice was husky with emotion. *'Eres toda para mí. Quiero estar contigo para siempre.'*

'Ramón.' She could feel heat at the back of her neck and her fingers tingled with adrenalin. *'Mi amor. Te quiero.'*

He stared at her for a moment. 'You speak Spanish?'

'Um…no.' The adrenalin buzz grew worse. This was like it had been with Andrew all over again. Why had she been so stupid? Saying the words had been bad enough. Saying them in Spanish had been a million times worse.

She stared at the floor. 'I, um, looked it up in a phrasebook. In the library.'

'You looked it up for *me*?'

The catch in his voice made her look up. Made her meet his gaze. And there was no censure, no ridicule or scorn in his eyes. Only wonder. And fear. And hope. 'Did you mean it?'

One little word. Three letters. It wasn't so hard to say, was it? Yet it stuck in her throat. If she said it, would she be making the worst mistake of her life?

'Jennifer? Did you mean it?'

She nodded.

'Say it again.'

It was more of a plea than a command. '*Te quiero*, Ramón,' she whispered. 'I love you.'

The fear vanished from his eyes, replaced with a deep, deep emotion. 'And I love you, Jennifer. To the depths of my soul.'

Three days later, a woman came onto the ward, a woman who looked so like Ramón that she had to be related to him, Jennifer thought.

'You are the senior sister on the ward?' the woman asked.

Jennifer nodded. 'Jennifer Jacobs,' she said.

The woman didn't return Jennifer's smile and ignored her proffered hand. 'I am Arabela Molinero. Dr Martínez is my brother. Is there somewhere private we can talk?'

A cold, nasty feeling began to creep its way up Jennifer's spine. 'Yes, of course. My office?' she suggested.

Arabela nodded curtly and followed her to her office. Jennifer closed the door behind them. 'May I offer you some coffee?'

'No, thank you.' Arabela's voice was barely polite. 'I saw my brother this morning.'

Ramón was on a late shift, so Jennifer had dropped him back at his flat this morning on her way in to work. Obviously Arabela had visited his flat.

'I need to talk to him about some family business but he has been very hard to contact recently. He never answers the phone. Nor even letters.' Arabela gave her a cool stare. 'And now I know why. I saw the photograph.'

'Photograph?'

'The two of you together. He keeps it in his wallet.'

Jennifer frowned. Why had Arabela been looking in Ramón's wallet? From the way she'd spoken, Ramón hadn't shown his sister the picture. Or maybe he had, and Jennifer was trying to see nuances in the conversation that weren't there. Arabela's command of English was good, but she wasn't speaking in her native tongue and the Spanish Jennifer had learned wasn't good enough for her to suggest switching the conversation to Spanish.

'And I saw the picture you drew.'

Picture? Jennifer flushed as she realised which picture Arabela meant. One of the first she'd drawn of Ramón, the one he'd asked if he could keep. 'Ah. That picture.'

'Yes. *That* picture. So you are lovers?'

Arabela clearly disapproved. Jennifer bit back the impulse to tell her that it was none of her business. This was Ramón's sister, so the very least she could do was be polite. Even if she didn't like the woman. 'Yes.'

Arabela made a scornful noise and Jennifer forgot her good intentions. 'Is there a problem?' she asked coolly.

'It depends on whether you consider Sofía a problem. Or perhaps your morals in England are not the same as ours in Spain.'

Jennifer frowned. 'I'm sorry, I don't have the faintest idea what you're talking about.'

'Sofía Villaneuva. Ramón's *novia*. His fiancée.'

His fiancée? But the night they'd first made love, Ramón

had been very explicit. *You're not betraying anyone with me. And I'm not betraying anyone with you.* He'd told her he was unattached.

Or had she simply misinterpreted it? Did he have a different moral standard—one that meant he could have a fiancée or a wife *and* a lover, and yet not be betraying anyone? Surely not. Arabela had virtually accused her of being a tart and not caring if she was sleeping with another woman's fiancé. And besides, Ramón wasn't like that. He wasn't a louse and a liar. Hadn't he promised her? Right at the start, he'd said he would never knowingly hurt her, that he would cherish her...

She felt dizzy, disorientated, as if someone had spun her around and around and around and suddenly let her go. This couldn't be happening. This really, really couldn't be happening.

'You did not know about Sofía?' This time, Arabela's voice was gentler. 'Then I am ashamed that my brother has behaved so badly.' She sighed. 'I am sorry to be the one to tell you. He has been betrothed to Sofía almost since he was born.'

Jennifer was too shocked to say anything.

'Our families have known each other for a long time. Their lands adjoin ours. Ramón is perhaps, as I think you call it here, sowing his wild oats. Travelling the world, being a doctor. But one day soon he will come back to Spain and give up hospital medicine, settle in to his position as the head of our family.'

'You're lying.' The words were out before Jennifer could stop them. Ramón had told her how important medicine was to him. He'd told her how much he loved working with children. He wouldn't give it all up just like that.

Arabela drew herself up to her full height and looked down her nose at Jennifer. 'I assure you, my family does not lie.'

Jennifer knew that tone well. Andrew had perfected it. Contempt, mixed with pride and anger. She fell back into her old habits of conciliation. 'Then there must be some mistake.'

'Yes. But the mistake is yours. Ramón does not belong here, and you do not belong in our world.'

Belatedly, Jennifer realised just how well Arabela Molinero was dressed, from her designer shoes through to her impeccable make-up. Her appearance simply screamed old money. And even when Ramón dressed in jeans and a casual shirt, his clothes looked expensive too. Much more discreetly so than his sister's, but Arabela had made her point. Ramón's family was rich, important—the complete opposite of her. So even if Ramón broke off his engagement for her, she would never fit into their world, never be part of his family. They would never accept her.

And even if Ramón broke off his engagement, could she ever trust him again? He had betrayed Sofía with her. He could just as easily betray *her* with the next woman who took his fancy.

How could she have been so stupid?

'I think I have said enough.'

Arabela's gaze had changed from contempt to pity. Strangely, that hurt even more. Jennifer lifted her chin. 'I agree. Excuse me, I have work to do.'

'Of course. I am sorry to have brought you bad news. My brother—'

'Is only here on secondment,' Jennifer cut in. 'And he will be leaving soon.'

'I see we are on the same wavelength. That is good,' Arabela said.

'Goodbye, Señora Molinero,' Jennifer said. 'I am sure you can find your own way out.'

Somehow she managed to focus on her work for the rest of the morning, though she was aware that all her movements were mechanical. She felt too sick to eat at lunch-time. Although she forced herself to go to the canteen and buy a sandwich, she left most of it because it tasted like ashes in her mouth.

Ramón was engaged.

Ramón was engaged to someone else.

Ramón was engaged to someone else and he'd lied to her about it.

The words kept beating round her head. On and on and on. He was the first man she'd trusted since Andrew, and he'd let her down in the worst possible way.

Worse still, she knew that by the time she came back from her lunch-break he'd be on duty. She'd have to face him, knowing that he was a liar and a cheat. Knowing that it was over between them. Knowing that all the sunshine in her life had been extinguished by three little words.

Ramón was engaged.

He was with a patient when she got back to the ward, and she managed to persuade Meg to do the ward round with him. She didn't want to see him yet—not until she'd composed herself, worked out what to do.

'Are you all right, JJ?' the other sister asked, concerned.

'Just a bit of a headache.' A huge headache. But not one that she wanted to share. 'I'll take a couple of paracetamol and I'll be fine. I'll just catch up with the paperwork—unless you want to do it?'

Meg pulled a face, just as Jennifer had anticipated. She knew that Meg hated paperwork even more than she did. 'Rather you than me,' Meg said feelingly.

'Yell if you need me,' Jennifer said, amazed at how well she was managing to pretend that everything was fine and her world hadn't really crashed into tiny pieces. She even managed to shift a fair quantity of paperwork—concentrating on something other than Ramón was the only way she could get through this without breaking down on the ward.

And then there was a rap on her door. Her stomach lurched. This was the moment of reckoning. She took a deep breath and prepared herself to face him.

'JJ, have you got a minute?' Lizzy asked as she opened the door.

Reprieve time. Jennifer relaxed. 'Sure. What can I do for you?'

'Dr Martínez asked me to fetch you—A and E have just sent up a little girl.'

Not a reprieve, then. But if the case was from A and E, she didn't have time to think of Ramón right now. And he wouldn't be thinking of her in romantic terms. Whatever she thought of him personally, professionally his conduct was impeccable. They would be concentrating on their patient, not each other. 'What's the problem?'

'A near-drowning.'

Jennifer was on her feet in an instant. 'Where is she?'

'Dr Martínez asked for her to be put in a side room—she's in room three.'

'What happened?' Jennifer asked as she walked over to room three with Lizzy.

'Apparently, she was playing out in the garden. Her mum answered the door and then her dad answered the phone—he thought it'd be all right because the little girl was nowhere near the paddling pool. The mum went back into the garden and saw the little girl face down in the pool.'

Jennifer could imagine the horror. Seeing your precious child floating lifelessly, thinking that your baby had died in the couple of minutes she'd been left alone, wondering why you hadn't just ignored the phone or the doorbell or whatever other distraction. Blaming yourself for your thoughtlessness, asking yourself why you hadn't taken the little one with you, why you hadn't done something different, why, why, why…

One of the worst risks of drowning was hypoxia, where not enough oxygen went to the body's tissues, which could lead to central nervous system damage.

'Jennifer.' Ramón looked at her in relief as she entered the room. 'Mr and Mrs Paget, this is Senior Sister Jacobs. She will be responsible for Tanya's care.'

'My baby.' Mrs Paget was white-faced, holding her daughter's hand tightly as if she would never let her go again. 'Please. Please, don't let me lose my baby.'

'We'll do our best, Mrs Paget.' Jennifer smiled reassuringly at her. 'I'm just going to have a word with Dr Martínez so he can tell me what happened in A and E and the care he'd like Tanya to have.'

'Tanya had a nasogastric tube to remove the water she'd swallowed. She was given 100 per cent oxygen in the ambulance and they brought her body temperature back up in A and E. No defibrillation needed,' Ramón told her swiftly. So at least the child didn't arrest. That was a good sign. 'I'd like Tanya on continuous pulse oximetry and I want her respiration monitored.'

Jennifer nodded. Fresh water caused disruption to the surfactant in the lungs—the chemicals secreted by the air sacs in the lungs that stopped the lungs collapsing when the child breathed out. They'd need to keep a close eye on Tanya to make sure that she didn't start suffering from acute respiratory distress syndrome, or ARDS—a life-threatening condition which could develop hours after her rescue if her lungs had been damaged. With ARDS, there wasn't enough surfactant and the lungs couldn't stay expanded. The effort of breathing would soon exhaust the child, and she might even stop breathing.

There was also a risk in the first twenty-four hours of sudden cerebral oedema developing—a build-up of fluid round the brain, which could cause headaches, vomiting and seizures. So she needed to keep a very close eye on little Tanya.

'What we're going to do,' she said to the Pagets, 'is put a little clip on Tanya's foot—it won't hurt her, but light goes through it to a probe which can tell us the oxygen levels in her blood, her pulse rate and her breathing. Sometimes children have breathing difficulties after a near-drowning, so we're just going to keep an eye on her.'

'I'm never going to let her out of my sight again,' Mrs Paget said. She glared at her husband. 'And neither is he.'

'These things happen,' Ramón said. 'Blaming each other won't help Tanya. She needs your support now. Lots of stories and cuddles, and just knowing her mum and dad are here.'

Mrs Paget flushed. 'I'm sorry. It's just when I think how we could have lost her…'

'I know. The might-have-beens are the worst. But try not to dwell on them. She's here with us now, so she's got a good chance.' Jennifer patted her arm. 'I'm on duty until teatime, and I'll be keeping an eye on Tanya until I leave. If you're worried about anything, come over to the nurses' station or press the buzzer by Tanya's bed.'

'Thank you.'

She did the first set of observations and recorded them on Tanya's chart. Ramón had left the room, so she crossed her fingers that he was with another patient.

Then she walked straight into him as she left the room.

CHAPTER NINE

'ARE you all right?' Ramón asked.

'Fine,' Jennifer lied.

'Meg said you had a headache.'

Yes, she did. And her headache was standing right in front of her. 'I've taken some paracetamol.'

He lowered his voice. 'Would you like me to bring a take-away home when I finish tonight, to save you cooking anything?'

'No, thanks.' Once it would have charmed her, but now it rankled that he'd called her cottage 'home'. The fact that he spent more time there than at his flat...well, that was in the past. It stopped right here, right now. She couldn't ever remember feeling this angry.

He frowned. 'Jennifer, is something wrong?'

How could he pretend like this? But, of course—he had no idea that she'd seen Arabela. That she knew the truth about him. She wanted to throw something at him, scream at him, stamp her feet or punch him... But it would only be temporary relief. And the gossip that would start when people saw her making a scene would be much, much worse. She reined in her temper and gave him a level stare. 'I had a visitor today. Arabela Molinero.'

'Ah.' He winced. 'My sister means well. But her manner... I hope she wasn't abrasive with you.'

'She was very honest.'

'I don't like the sound of that.' He glanced at his watch. 'I can take a break when your shift ends. We'll go for a walk and talk about it then.'

'There's no point.'

'I think there is.'

He reached out to touch her but she pulled back. What she wanted right now was for him to hold her, to stroke her hair and tell her everything would be fine. But it was way too late for that. And if he touched her now, she'd lose her resolve. She couldn't afford that to happen.

'*No te preocupes.* It will be all right,' he said softly.

She wanted to believe him. She really, really wanted to believe him. But after what she knew now, how could it ever be the same again between them?

'We need to talk in private. I'll meet you in the garden by the fountain,' he said. 'Two hours.'

The next one hundred and twenty-three minutes dragged by slowly. Every set of observations she did was uneventful, every patient was sleeping or busy being entertained by parents and siblings, and every second felt like a lifetime. The one good point was that Ramón kept well out of her way.

Finally, she was able to do her handover. And when she walked over to the fountain in the hospital grounds after her shift, Ramón was the only person sitting on one of the benches.

'Jennifer.' Again he reached for her hand as she sat down, and again she pulled back.

He sighed. 'All right. Tell me the bad news. What did Arabela say?'

'You didn't tell me your family was rich.'

'You never asked.'

Fair point. But they hadn't really talked about families, except when she'd told him that she was alone in the world. He hadn't mentioned his family at all, and she'd assumed he was simply being sensitive about her own lack of family.

He regarded her seriously. 'Does it make a difference to us, my family's money?'

'You have duties, as the head of your family.'

He slapped his forehead. 'I should have guessed Arabela would try to interfere. I once told you, *querida*, how important medicine is to me. My family likes to think I'll come back to the fold—but they know in their hearts that I won't. I'm a doctor first and foremost. And that's why I don't practise medicine in Sevilla. They drive me mad with their constant demands about family business and the duties of the eldest son. Since my father died, Arabela and my mother think I have a social position to keep up.' He grimaced. 'I hate all that. All the cocktail parties and the chatter and the hidden knives. The dirty looks and poisonous whispers if you're not wearing the right labels, driving the right sort of car, serving the most expensive wine. That's not how I want to live.' He shook his head in disgust. 'My younger brother Pablo is perfectly capable of running the family estates. He *likes* doing it. And he doesn't mind the social expectations that go with it. So why should I go back and displace him, making us both unhappy?'

Had she not known the rest of it, Jennifer would have sympathised with him. Agreed with him. As it was… 'Sofía Villaneuva,' she said softly.

He stared at her. 'What about her?'

'What about her?' she asked, outraged. How could he possibly dismiss his fiancée like that? 'Ramón, you lied to me. You said you were free. And all the time you were betrothed to Sofía.'

'You think I would…?' He shook his head in amazement. 'Does what we shared mean nothing to you?'

Answering a question with a question. Two could play at that. 'Are you engaged to her?'

'I can't believe you think—'

'Are you engaged to her?' she repeated coldly.

Ramón folded his arms. 'There's only one woman I am going to marry, Jennifer Jacobs. And I'm sitting right next to her.'

He assumed that she was going to marry him? But he'd never even asked her! And he was going back to Spain—his secondment finished in a little over a week. And he *still* hadn't answered her question. 'I want a yes-or-no answer, Ramón. Are you engaged to Sofía Villaneuva?'

He winced. 'It's complicated.'

'Yes or no?'

He rested his right ankle on his left knee and drummed his fingers on it. 'Technically.'

'Technically?' She stared at him in disbelief. 'How the *hell* can you be engaged to someone "technically"? Either you are or you aren't.'

'It isn't what you think.'

'No? You're here for four months on secondment, your fiancée doesn't come with you, and you're bored so you have a tawdry little affair with an insignificant nurse who won't make a fuss when it's over!'

'That's not how it is between us, and you know it.'

'Yeah, right. More like you were thinking with another part of your anatomy instead of your head. You told me what I wanted to hear so you could get me into your bed. And I fell for it—hook, line and bloody sinker!' She clenched her fists. 'How could you do that to me?'

'Jennifer, listen to me. It's not what it seems. I love you.'

She stood up. 'No, you don't. I'm just your cheap little bit on the side, a way of passing the time until you go back to Spain.'

'That's not true.' He stood up and tried to take her hand but she slapped his hand, hard.

'Don't touch me, you bastard! You lied to me. You made love to me when you were engaged to someone else. Even if you break it off with her now, how can I ever trust you? I'll always be wondering when you'll do the same to me. And it will be *when*, not *if*, Ramón. I've met your sort before.'

'I'm not a cheat, and I would never, ever betray you.'

'You already have. You cheated on Sofía and you lied to me, Ramón.'

'A lie of omission. I didn't tell you about Sofía because it's…complicated.' And there were things he still couldn't tell her. Secrets that weren't his to tell. 'Jennifer, I can explain—'

'What? That you're a liar and a cheat? The worst thing, Ramón, is that your sister actually *pitied* me. And she was right, because I was stupid enough to be taken in by you.'

'So you're not going to listen to my side of the story?' he demanded.

'And what? Hear more lies?'

'No. The truth.' Or as much of it as he could tell her. 'I've known Sofía virtually all my life. Her parents own the vineyard next to my family's. Our parents were friends as well as neighbours and business rivals. Sofía and I played together from the moment we could sit up. Our mothers decided it would be a good idea that the firstborn Martínez and the firstborn Villanueva should marry. It's…I don't know, a dynasty sort of thing. Everyone expected it. Except we're not in love with each other. Never have been, never will be.'

'So why are you still engaged to her?'

'We were just waiting for the right time to break it off. She lives in Madrid and I've been on secondment in England for a while. We've been hoping our families will get used to the idea of us not being together.' Though clearly it hadn't worked—Arabela at least was still convinced that her brother was going to marry Sofía.

'Why don't you just tell them the truth?'

Because the truth wasn't his to tell. 'It's not easy to break family obligations.'

'I wouldn't know about that,' she said tightly.

'*Cariña*, that's not what I mean. I'm not throwing your family history back at you. Maybe it's a Spanish thing. Look, we can work this out.'

'No. You kept something this big from me—what else aren't you telling me?'

Too much. But he couldn't break Sofía's trust. He'd promised. 'I love you. Isn't that enough?'

'No, it bloody well isn't! How can I trust you? How can I be sure that you're not going to tell me lies in the future— that you're not going to fall in love with someone else and forget that you're involved with *me*?'

'I wouldn't do that.'

'Too right. Because you're not going to get the chance. I don't want to see you again, Ramón. Ever, ever again,' she yelled. 'If there's anything of yours at my house, I'll have it couriered over to you. And if there's anything of mine at your flat, just throw it away. I don't want it back.'

'Jennifer, you're angry and upset and I can understand that.'

'Don't you *dare* patronise me!' So he *was* like Andrew after all.

'I'm not trying to patronise you. This is all a mess and I know it's my fault, but we can sort it out. Work it out *together*.'

'I can't trust you any more, Ramón. And without trust we don't have a future.' She knew that her heart was going to break. But if she didn't do this now, it'd hurt a lot more in the future. The future—when his family wanted an heir and they found out about her background, and just like Andrew they would think she wasn't the right one to provide Ramón with an heir. Arabela had made it clear she would never accept Jennifer in her brother's life. And Jennifer knew what it was like to grow up without a family, so she couldn't part Ramón from his. He would go back to

Spain and do his duty and marry Sofía, and that was how it had to be.

It felt as if her mouth was full of sawdust but she managed to say the hardest word of all. 'Goodbye.'

It wasn't until much, much later that evening that Jennifer finally cried—when she went to bed and discovered that it was much too big without Ramón. And even though she'd changed the sheets, she could still smell his scent. She could still remember how it felt to fall asleep in his arms, held close and cherished, listening to his heartbeat. And she missed him.

But she could never trust him again. Like Andrew, Ramón believed that he was right about everything. He expected to get his own way all the time—even believed it was his due. She'd spent four years as Andrew's wife, and more than twice as long picking up the pieces again afterwards. And just when she'd thought it was time to start living again, she'd chosen exactly the same sort of man. Proud, arrogant, sure of himself. A man who would give no quarter. A Spaniard.

However much her heart missed Ramón, she had to follow her head. It was over. Completely and utterly over. And she would never, ever make the same mistake again.

The next morning, Jennifer awoke with a raging headache and puffy eyes. She was on a late so she took a paracetamol and bathed her eyes in cold water. Spider prowled round the house, as if looking for something. Looking for *someone*.

Jennifer sighed. 'Spider, I know you liked him. But we were both wrong about him. He's not for us. It's over, and he's not coming back.'

The cat leapt onto her lap and snuggled into her. She stroked his soft fur and let the tears fall again. 'He'll go back to Spain in a few days, and then I won't have to see him again. We'll be fine on our own, just you and me.'

Though she knew in her heart it wasn't true.

Ramón was in clinic when she did the handover at the beginning of her shift. She did the ward rounds with one of the registrars, then stayed out of Ramón's way for the rest of his shift, making sure she was busy with patients whenever he was on the ward. Little Tanya had recovered enough to be discharged—his signature was on the discharge note, she noticed, and he'd written a letter to the GP. And added a note for the parents, giving them signs to watch for.

Such a good, thorough doctor. A man she could respect professionally. If only he'd been the same in his personal life…

He didn't bother coming to see her before he left at the end of his shift and she wasn't sure whether she was more hurt than relieved. Probably both, she admitted wryly. If he'd made a single move towards her, she knew her resolve would have weakened.

'We're having a whip-round,' Lizzy said a couple of days later, rattling an envelope at her. 'For Dr Martínez. He's leaving on Friday.'

'Right. I'd forgotten.' It was a lie. Jennifer knew exactly how many seconds it was until he left Brad's. Until he left her life for ever. She rummaged in her purse and put some money into the envelope.

'Thanks, JJ.' Lizzy smiled at her. 'Any ideas what we can get him?'

'I don't know.' At Lizzy's obvious surprise, she flinched. So much for thinking she'd been discreet. The whole hospital probably knew she'd had a wild fling with the dashing Spanish doctor—and that they'd split up. Or maybe not.

Lizzy wasn't tactless or malicious, and if she'd had any idea what had happened between Jennifer and Ramón, she would never have asked the question. 'I'm out of ideas today,' she said, forcing herself to smile. 'Try asking Meg. Or Neil—he'll have a bloke's perspective on it.'

'Rightio.'

Lizzy was still hovering and Jennifer frowned. 'What's up?'

'Well—I was just going to ask if you were all right. You look a bit off colour.'

Again, Jennifer forced a smile to her face. 'Thanks for the concern, but I'm fine.' Just nursing a broken heart.

A heart that definitely wasn't healing, she thought later that day when she looked down at the pad where she'd been making notes in a staff meeting and all she'd done had been to doodle. Well, maybe a little more than doodle: she'd been sketching. From memory. Ramón, curled up with Spider on the sofa and sharing an illicit packet of tortilla chips with the cat. Ramón, blowing a kiss. Ramón, laughing.

She shredded the evidence and flushed it down the toilet. And then she was violently sick.

Oh, great. A stomach bug was the last thing she needed right now. Though on the plus side it would mean she'd miss Ramón's last day. She wouldn't have to be there and watch him leave. Watch him walk away from her.

She washed her face and cleaned her teeth, then drank a glass of water. Perhaps it wasn't a bug. Perhaps it was because she was stressed out to the max. She needed a holiday. Though it certainly wouldn't be in the Mediterranean. Nowhere near orange groves. Maybe a few days on the coast at Yorkshire, looking for ammonites and paddling in the sea, would help her get her perspective back.

A lonely holiday. Doing the kind of things Ramón would have loved to share with her. Except he'd have added the touches she would leave out—going to the fair, eating candyfloss and hot sugary doughnuts, sitting on the pier to eat fish and chips and throw titbits to the seagulls, walking along the beach hand in hand at sunset, exploring Gothic ruins and scaring each other silly with ghostly tales...

'Stop,' she told herself sternly. 'You're only making it worse. Just let it go.'

The next two days were spent being civil to each other in front of patients and other staff, and keeping out of each other's way as much as possible. Several times she thought he was going to say something to her, but she turned away. What could he say? All the apologies in the world couldn't make it right again.

Jennifer wasn't sure what was worse—home, where the house seemed empty and Spider was pining for Ramón, or work, where she could bump into him at any time.

'You'll get over it,' she told herself. 'You survived Andrew. You'll survive this too.' But the words seemed hollow. And right now she felt lousy. Tired all the time—probably because she wasn't sleeping properly, and the strain was making her feel nauseous.

'Work,' she said firmly. 'Concentrate on work, Jennifer.' At least she was rostered to the paediatric assessment unit this morning, so she wouldn't have to do the ward round with Ramón.

Her fourth case was the one that set alarm bells ringing. Kevin Myers sat quietly—listlessly, even—while she talked to his mum.

'I thought it was just a bug going round—he's had a headache and a bit of a sore throat.' Mrs Myers looked anxious. 'And then he got this rash on his feet. I thought it was athlete's foot but the chemist said it wasn't and I ought to bring him to see you.'

'Athlete's foot is usually between the toes,' Jennifer said.

'The skin's red and flaky, and sometimes you'll see little brown blisters. Plus they itch like mad. Trust me, if it was that, you'd know about it. Can you take your socks off for me, Kevin, and let me see the rash?' she asked.

The boy sighed and did as she asked. The rash was round, about five centimetres wide, and reddened on the outside with a paler section in the centre. Definitely not athlete's foot. It looked more like Lyme disease, she thought. Though the condition was rare in the Midlands— it was more prevalent in the south of the country.

'Can you roll your tracksuit bottoms up a bit, please— just above your knees?' she asked Kevin.

He nodded and did so. Jennifer examined his knees, and found the signs she'd been hoping not to see—slight swelling and redness.

'And now can I have a look at your neck?' As she'd half expected, the glands in his neck were slightly swollen.

'Have you been anywhere on holiday in the last two months?' she asked.

'No. But Kevin went on a school trip to the New Forest,' Mrs Myers said.

The south. Tick country. 'When?' Jennifer asked.

'Well over a month ago.'

Jennifer nodded. 'Can you remember being bitten by an insect at all, Kevin?'

The little boy shrugged. 'I dunno.'

Not all children remembered being bitten, plus tick bites were painless and didn't itch, unlike other insect bites. 'I'm going to need a blood test,' she said. 'I think Kevin may have been bitten by a tick, and that's given him something called Lyme disease.'

'Is it serious?' Mrs Myers asked.

'It can be if you don't treat it. But if the blood tests show I'm right, we can give Kevin antibiotics which will clear it up.' She took a blood sample and labelled it. 'I'll get this off to the lab. If you'd like to come back in a couple of hours, I'll get a doctor to see you.'

'Thank you.'

When the results came back, she went through to the ward to find Neil. 'He's on a break,' Lizzy said when Jennifer asked if she'd seen Neil. 'But Dr Martínez is here.'

Ramón came out of a side room. 'Did you want something, Lizzy?'

'No, but JJ does.' The student smiled at her. 'PAU case.'

Jennifer deliberately focused on her outbreath, keeping it slow and even. There was nothing to get worked up about. She'd known that Neil might be on a break or busy, so she'd have to deal with Ramón. Luck wasn't on her side today. Well, they were professionals. The patient had to come first. 'I've got a ten-year-old patient in PAU with a round erythematous rash on his foot, clear in the centre. He's got joint swelling, headaches, lethargy—and the glands in his neck are up. He can't remember being bitten by an insect, but he went to the New Forest over a month ago, and it's one of the more common areas for ticks.'

'So you think it's Lyme disease?'

She handed Ramón the blood test results. 'His white blood cell count is up and so's his erythrocyte sedimentation rate.'

'That's pretty conclusive.'

'Can you write him up for antibiotics, please?'

'Of course. Your patient is in the assessment unit now?'

She nodded.

'Then I will come with you. Bleep me if you need me, Lizzy.'

They walked along the corridor together in an uneasy silence. When they reached the unit, Jennifer introduced him to Kevin and Mrs Myers.

Ramón checked the rash himself, and nodded. 'The blood tests suggest Lyme disease, and the rash clinches it for me. It's caused by corkscrew-shaped bacteria called spirochetes, which are transmitted by ticks when they sink their jaws into your skin. Ticks are very small so you don't always see them—and the bite doesn't hurt or itch afterwards so you don't always realise you have been bitten. It's easy to miss and it's very common among walkers,' he said. 'Mrs Myers, is Kevin allergic to penicillin at all?'

'No, but his dad is.'

There was a possibility that Kevin had inherited his father's allergy. 'Then, to be on the safe side, I will prescribe a different antibiotic.' Ramón wrote out a prescription. 'He needs to take this three times a day for two weeks, and make sure he finishes the course—even if the rash looks better before then.'

Mrs Myers nodded.

'Now, Sister Jacobs tells me that Kevin's knees are inflamed. We can give him ibuprofen to stop the swelling and any pain, but there should be no permanent damage to his joints. If you notice any other symptoms or it doesn't clear up, go back to your GP—I will write a note explaining what has happened and what I've prescribed.'

'Thank you, Doctor.'

Jennifer noticed that Mrs Myers was smiling much more broadly now—and not just with relief that her son would be fine. Women always smiled like that when they were with Ramón.

'Kevin, your body has developed antibodies but they will not prevent you from getting Lyme disease again. The only way to prevent it is to make sure you're not bitten by ticks again. You need to wear long trousers and tuck them into your socks, and put insect repellent on your socks and shoes. Ticks like dark places and hair, so get someone to check your scalp, neck and armpit when you've been outside.'

He turned to Mrs Myers. 'If you see a tick, pull it off.

Grip it close to the skin with a pair of tweezers and pull it steadily and gently upward. Don't twist, or you will break the head off. If the head stays in the skin, take it out with a sterile needle as if it was a splinter.'

'Yes, Doctor.'

He winked at Kevin. 'You'll be playing football again and being cheeky to your mum before you know it.'

Jennifer slipped away while he was still talking to his patients. She was relieved to find that she had a few more cases—at least it meant she wouldn't have to be alone with Ramón. And she wouldn't be tempted to beg him to hold her, make her forget all the unpleasantness. She just had to hold out for a few more days...

Ramón's last day was unbearable. At least they weren't on the same shift so the torture wasn't that prolonged. She signed his card with a simple 'Good luck in your new job, JJ' and stayed well to the back of the crowd when Neil gave Ramón the new briefcase and bottle of good wine Lizzy had bought with the whip-round.

And then his shift was over. He walked off the ward and out of her life. She knew he was buying drinks for everyone in the bar across the road—the place where the ward staff always held their leaving or celebration drinks—but she couldn't face going to the party when her shift ended. Instead, she went home. It was a miserable drive. As soon as she switched the radio on, she heard 'Ain't No Sunshine'. The song suited her mood but the words were way too close to home. She changed stations again and again, but all the pop stations seemed to be playing songs about love affairs gone wrong, and all the classical ones were playing music she associated with Ramón. The chamber music they'd gone to see together and, even worse, the piece he'd played for her on his guitar the night they'd first made love.

At the time she'd thought the good memories would push away all the bad ones. She'd had no idea that good memories could hurt just as much.

Ramón looked at his watch. Jennifer should be here by now. Her shift had ended half an hour ago. Unless... Maybe there had been an emergency on the ward and she hadn't been able to get away.

He excused himself from the crowd and went outside where it was quieter. He dialled Jennifer's direct line on his mobile and waited.

'Paediatrics, Sister Moran speaking,' a voice informed him.

His heart sank. Sally Moran was one of the worst of the gossipmongers. If he wasn't very careful about what he said, he'd be leaving Jennifer to the mercy of the hospital grapevine. 'Hi, Sally. It's Ramón. I'm sorry you can't make the party tonight. I just wanted to check that the *tapas* I left was all right.'

'It's fine. And it's really sweet of you to think of the night staff.'

'*De nada.* Not at all.' He paused. 'Tell the stragglers from the late shift to hurry up or this lot will have drunk the bar dry.'

'There aren't any stragglers,' she said. 'Everyone's with you.'

'OK. I just wanted to check. Take care.'

'You, too.'

He cut the connection. Hell. He'd been counting on the fact that Jennifer's good manners would make her come to his leaving party. As the most senior nurse on the ward, she should have been there. But clearly she'd decided not to come.

He shook his head in frustration. What was the use of pride, if it was keeping him from the woman he loved? He dialled her home number. It rang once, twice, three times. And then the answering-machine kicked in. 'Hello, I can't take your call right now. Leave a message after the beep and I'll call you back.'

He only hoped she would.

'Jennifer, *mi amor*, if you're there, pick up the phone.'

He waited. Nothing.

'OK. When you get in, ring me. Please.' He took a deep breath and pushed his pride away. 'I miss you. I understand why you don't want to be here at the party, but I miss you. I have missed you every second since…' He sighed. 'My plane goes tomorrow morning.' He gave her the flight number and the time. 'Please. If you don't want to see me tonight, at least come to the airport tomorrow. I don't want to go without holding you one more time.' He didn't want to go, full stop. But there were a few things that needed sorting out in Spain. Fast. 'I—' There was a long beep, and he cursed. Why did answering-machines never give you enough time to leave a proper message? 'I love you, Jennifer,' he said softly into the silence. *'Te quiero. Siempre.'*

He only hoped she knew that.

Jennifer didn't bother checking her answering-machine when she got home. She wasn't expecting any messages. Besides, all she really wanted was a long, soothing bath.

It wasn't until the next morning that she noticed the light flashing and played the message back. She stopped breathing when she heard Ramón's voice, heard his message.

He wanted her to go to the airport. She glanced at the clock. She could make it if she left right now. She could go to him and know that he'd be waiting for her with open arms.

But she would always wonder. If Ramón was late home,

suspicion would start to gnaw at her. And although she loved him, it wasn't enough. Not without trust. Suspicion and fear and jealousy would eat her love away. She'd been there before and she wasn't going there again. Not for anything.

Holding the tears in check—only just—she deleted his message.

'Last call. Last call for flight number…'

Ramón looked wildly round the departure hall. There was no sign of Jennifer. And there had been no messages waiting for him at the check-in desk, nothing relayed over the loudspeaker. Either she hadn't received his message…or she didn't care enough.

As he strode towards the plane, having completed the formalities, his heart splintered. Because now he knew the worst. Jennifer simply didn't love him enough. And he would just have to live with that.

CHAPTER TEN

THREE weeks. Three miserable, dragging weeks. Even though Jennifer knew Ramón had gone for good—and that she was better off without him anyway—she still found herself listening for his voice on the ward, just in case he'd decided to come back. *Just in case he'd come back for her.* She was still sleeping badly, which accounted for the tiredness and twinges of nausea. But when she couldn't face the cup of coffee Meg made her one morning and realised into the bargain that her period was late, Jennifer began to wonder.

She couldn't be pregnant. She couldn't *possibly* be pregnant. She and Ramón had always used protection, even that time he'd made love to her under the stars in her garden.

But the only form of contraception that was one hundred per cent guaranteed was abstinence. And during their affair they hadn't been able to get enough of each other. They'd barely been able to keep their hands off each other on the ward—and once outside the hospital, they hadn't bothered trying. They'd touched, tasted...

She bit back a whimper as the loss hit her yet again. When would her heart start listening to her head? When would it realise she'd done the right thing?

She kept her panic to herself, managed to get through the rest of her shift, then picked up a pregnancy test from the supermarket on the way home. Two minutes after she got indoors, she was looking at the test stick, willing the result to be negative.

Her hands were shaking so much she could hardly see the little windows on the test. A blue line appeared in the first window, to tell her that the test was working. So far, so good. 'Please, be clear,' she muttered desperately to the second window. '*Please*. Please, be clear.'

But a faint blue line appeared. A line which grew steadily darker before her horrified gaze.

She was pregnant. Pregnant with Ramón's baby.

She dropped the test stick and was promptly sick.

An hour later, when she'd washed her face and had a glass of water and picked at a sandwich, she sat curled on the sofa with Spider on her lap. 'Oh, *gatito*.' Without even realising it, she used Ramón's endearment for the cat. 'What am I going to do?'

Of course, we can't have children. Andrew's voice echoed in her head. *I know, Petal, it's disappointing—but we can't risk it. We don't know anything about your family.*

When she'd done her nursing training, she'd learned a lot about genetics, and had realised Andrew had had a point. A very strong point. They'd had no idea if she was a carrier for an incurable disease such as Huntingdon's chorea or Alzheimer's. She thought back to the Stewarts and little Keiran—she, too, might have a baby with cystic fibrosis. If she and Ramón were both carriers...

She took a deep breath. No. She couldn't panic yet. And the test might be wrong. She might not be pregnant at all.

Then she smiled wryly. Who was she trying to kid? Home tests nowadays were as accurate as the ones they used at the hospital. As for the tiredness and nausea, they were common early symptoms of pregnancy—symptoms which she'd misread and put down to stress. She was pregnant all right. But *how* pregnant?

She thought hard. She'd missed her last period as well as this one. But she'd put that down to stress after breaking up with Ramón. The period before that had been lighter than usual, so it could have been breakthrough bleeding, before the pregnancy hormones had kicked in. So she was somewhere between eight and twelve weeks. It was still early enough to have a...

No. Her mind recoiled from the word. She didn't want a termination. This baby might be unexpected, but she wanted it. Wanted it with a fierce, protective hunger that surprised her with its intensity.

Morally, she knew she should let Ramón know. She didn't want anything from him—she was quite capable of supporting herself and the baby—but he had a right to know that he was going to be a father. She'd see her GP, find out when the baby was due, and tell him later.

'I'd say you're about...' Bernie Pitt felt her abdomen gently '...twelve weeks.' He smiled at her. 'Congratulations.'

'Thanks.' Jennifer took a deep breath. 'So where do we go from here?'

'I'll get you booked in for a dating scan at Brad's, just to confirm your due date, and then we can think about doing the triple test when you're fifteen weeks. Would it be easier for you to have your antenatal appointments at the hospital, so you could just pop down from work, or would you rather see the midwife here?'

'Here, I think.' Where at least people wouldn't be gossiping about her.

'All right. I'll book you in with Jill for three weeks' time.' He took a leaflet from his desk. 'Read this and it should answer most of your questions about the triple test. It's a screening test and you're not obliged to have it—it's really up to you.'

Jennifer took a deep breath. 'I don't know anything about my family medical history—I wasn't brought up by my parents and my birth mother was dead by the time I traced her.'

'Well, I hope you're not sitting there worrying about all

the terrible diseases you could be passing on.' Bernie gave her a reassuring smile. 'You're a paediatric nurse so you see the worst of things—but you also know you're not seeing everyday cases. Most babies are absolutely fine. The chances of you having a genetic disorder are very, very low.'

She nodded politely, though she wasn't completely convinced. There was a patch of heat at the back of her neck, and a little voice whispering in her head, *What if? What if?* A little voice that became Andrew's. *We don't know what's in your family.*

'I'll book your scan now, if you don't mind waiting a couple of minutes.' At her nod, he rang the antenatal clinic to book an ultrasound slot. 'Eight-thirty on Thursday morning OK with you?' he asked, with his hand over the mouthpiece.

Jennifer checked her diary. 'Fine. I'm on a late.'

'Good.' He confirmed the appointment and hung up. 'Jill will be in touch about your first antenatal—but if you're worried about anything in the meantime, just ring the surgery.'

'Thanks.' It felt odd to be a patient. Jennifer couldn't even remember the last time she'd been ill. She only ever came to the surgery for regular smear tests and vaccination boosters.

And visiting the hospital as a patient felt even stranger. Luckily there was no one she knew in the antenatal clinic, so she simply checked in at Reception and waited for her scan.

'Is this your first baby?' the sonographer asked.

'Yes.'

'Ah, what a shame the dad couldn't be here. They love this bit.' She smiled brightly. 'But I can do you a photo if you like, so you can show him later. And there's always the second scan.'

Jennifer had to fight the tears back. She couldn't afford to think about how Ramón would have reacted to seeing his baby on the screen. 'Thank you,' she said, just about managing to keep her self-control.

'At least the gel's warm here,' the sonographer said with a grin. 'That's the difference between us and the midwives.'

Jennifer lay back and bared her abdomen for the conductive gel. Then the sonographer ran the head of the machine over her belly and paused. 'There we go.'

This time Jennifer couldn't hold the tears back at the first sight of her baby.

The sonographer handed her a wad of tissues. 'I know. I've done this for years, and the first sight still gets me every time—seeing this little miracle wriggling about.' She measured the crown to rump length and the femur on screen, then the circumference of the head and abdomen. 'Yep, you're definitely around twelve and a half weeks.'

'Is…is everything all right?' Jennifer asked.

'Everything looks fine. See, there's the heart beating.' The sonographer pointed it out on the screen. 'Two arms, two legs, that's the spine and the ribcage, and that's the bladder. Nice and full. Actually, that's a good picture. Would you like me to take this one?'

'Please.'

'How many? One for your man and one for your mum as well?'

'Just one,' Jennifer said softly. There was a lump in her throat the size of a brick. She didn't have a partner to share this with, or a mum to cluck over her during her pregnancy and knit bootees and reminisce about how she'd felt during her own pregnancy. Jennifer would never know if her mother had had morning sickness, if she'd had any cravings, if she'd been convinced Jennifer was a boy or a girl, what other names she'd thought of. No one to look at the baby and say, 'Oh, yes, Jennifer, she's got your dad's nose,' or, 'She's got my mum's chin,' or…

'Are you OK?' the sonographer asked.

'Just a bit hormonal,' Jennifer said, rubbing away a tear with the back of her hand. She'd spent over thirty years without a mother. She should be used to it by now.

'Well, you just relax and enjoy the baby.' The sonographer winked. 'Put your feet up and make your man run around after you for a bit.'

Jennifer made a noncommittal noise. Ramón certainly wouldn't be running about after her. He was in another country. Right now he didn't actually know she was pregnant. And when he did find out…there was no guarantee he'd want anything to do with her.

'So, we'll see you again at twenty weeks, then.'

Jennifer had done enough reading to know that was the major anomaly scan. 'Yes. And you want me to drink about four glasses of water before the scan so you can get a clear picture.'

The sonographer chuckled. 'Oh, no. We're *much* meaner to staff. Make that five glasses!'

Jennifer smiled back, knowing that the woman was teasing. She tucked the baby's photograph into her handbag and went for a long walk. Now her pregnancy had been confirmed and she knew the due date, she really had to tell Ramón. Though how was she going to get in touch with him? All she knew was that his family lived somewhere near Seville. International Directory Enquiries would need something a lot more specific. She had no idea of his address, whether he lived with his family and his number was listed under his own name or his father's name, or even if his phone number was listed.

She lingered over a cup of hot chocolate. Although it brought back memories of Ramón, at least she could drink it—she couldn't even stand the smell of coffee at the moment. And then she walked slowly back to the hospital and headed for Personnel.

'I'm sorry, we can't give out personal information,' the receptionist said.

'I understand, but...' Jennifer took a deep breath. 'There's something he needs to know. Something really, really important. If I wrote a letter to him, would you be able to forward it for me? That way, you wouldn't be breaking any rules because you wouldn't have told me his address.'

'I don't know.'

'Please.'

Something of her desperation must have communicated itself to the receptionist, who sighed. 'All right.'

'I'll bring it in tomorrow morning,' Jennifer promised.

She was slightly early for her shift, but no one commented. Meg accepted her excuse of 'doing a detox' when Jennifer refused a cup of coffee at break-time, and Jennifer managed to get through all her admin without a single hiccup.

Until Mandy and Paul Knights brought little Stephen to the ward. He had recovered well from the operation to fix his cleft palate. 'We were seeing the speech therapist,' Mandy said, 'so we thought we'd come in and show off our boy.'

'Hello, gorgeous.' Jennifer held her arms out for a cuddle, breathing in his soft baby smell. 'How's he doing?'

'Really well,' Paul said. 'I can hardly believe it. No problems with feeding, no infection or anything.'

'Is Dr Martínez around?' Mandy asked.

Jennifer steeled herself. 'I'm afraid he's no longer with us.' She was amazed at how calm she sounded, considering how churned-up she felt inside.

'That's a shame.' Mandy frowned, and then beamed.

'I've got to tell someone, or I'll burst! JJ, we're expecting again. I'm about eight weeks.'

'Congratulations,' Jennifer said automatically, though inside she was crying. She was pregnant, too. And nobody was going to congratulate her. Everyone was going to be talking about her, whispering about how stupid she'd been.

'I think it's a boy. And we're going to call him Martin, after Dr Martínez,' Mandy said with a smile.

'Martina, if it's a girl,' Paul added.

'I'm sure he'd be pleased,' Jennifer said. He'd love the idea of a baby being named after him.

Though how was he going to react to the news that he was going to be a father?

Jennifer wrote the letter that night and gave it to the clerk in Personnel before her shift the next day. And then she waited. And waited.

At first she put it down to the international post taking longer than domestic post.

Then she wondered if maybe the letter hadn't been forwarded. A discreet enquiry disabused her of that idea—the clerk had posted it the same day Jennifer had handed it to her.

And as the days slipped into weeks, Jennifer realised that Ramón simply wasn't going to reply to her letter. He didn't want to know.

She cupped her abdomen. 'Well, we don't need him,' she told the gentle swell of her bump. 'I've got love enough for two. And I promise you, you'll always have me.' Whatever desperation had driven her own mother to desert her, Jennifer knew she would never do that to her own child.

She was just putting down some dust sheets on her day off, ready to start decorating her spare bedroom for a nursery, when the phone rang. 'Hello, JJ. It's Jill.'

The midwife? 'Hi, Jill,' she said carefully, trying not to panic.

'How are you feeling?'

'Fine.' Apart from the hot feeling at the back of her neck. The feeling that told her something was wrong. Badly wrong.

'I've got your test results back.'

'They're OK, aren't they?' Jennifer asked, knowing full well that they weren't. The midwife wouldn't have phoned if the results were fine.

'Remember we discussed how the test screened for alpha-foetal protein in your blood, and the levels were measured against your age? I'm pleased to say that your Down's risk is well within the normal range.'

Jennifer began to shake. 'And spina bifida?' She hadn't been planning to have a baby. She hadn't been taking folic acid supplements before she'd fallen pregnant and for the first three months to help prevent neural tube defects. Spina bifida, where one or more of the vertebrae in the baby's spine didn't develop properly so it left the spinal cord exposed, was a possibility.

'I'm afraid that one's not so good,' Jill said gently. 'Now, remember that it's only a screening test. It doesn't mean your baby absolutely, definitely has a problem. A lot of the time in screen positive results, the baby's fine. You don't have to have an amniocentesis.'

'But you'd advise it.'

'If you want a definite result one way or the other, yes.'

She'd come this far. She'd even thought she'd felt a flutter in her stomach, as if tiny butterflies were moving their wings or as if someone was blowing bubbles through a straw. No way was she going to lose this baby now. 'Whatever happens, I'm keeping the baby.'

'That's entirely up to you. No one's going to judge you at all, JJ. I'm here to support you, whatever you decide.'

'OK. I'll have the amnio—but only so I know one way or the other. Even if my baby has spina bifida, I'm not having a termination.'

'I'll book it for you and ring you back with the appointment time,' Jill said. 'Do you want me to come with you?'

'Thanks for the offer, but I'll be fine.'

'What about getting home afterwards? You need a couple of days just resting, and I wouldn't advise you to drive yourself. Apart from increasing the risk of a miscarriage, you're going to be upset and it'll be difficult to concentrate,' Jill pointed out.

'I'll get a taxi,' Jennifer said.

She replaced the receiver and sat with her head in her hands. Spina bifida. She knew enough from her experience on Paediatrics that the severity varied, depending on how much nerve tissue was exposed. The number of cases had dropped, mainly due to women taking vitamin supplements from the moment they started trying to conceive, but even so three babies in ten thousand were born with it.

In the worst-case scenario, it could be myelocele, where the spinal cord was malformed and the baby's legs were paralysed. There was also a greater risk of cerebral palsy and kidney damage. Meningocoele was less severe, when the nerve tissue of the spinal cord was intact but the membranes surrounding it protruded. Surgery meant that the baby stood a better chance. The best outcome would be spina bifida occulta, the most common form of spina bifida, where the bony arches behind the spinal cord didn't grow together properly but the baby could live a relatively normal life.

Right then she wasn't sure whether it was better to know as much as she did or to be completely in the dark.

'It's a screening test,' she reminded herself. 'It's not a definite. There's probably nothing to worry about. Stop panicking.'

And then she froze as the doorbell sounded. She wasn't expecting visitors. She shook herself. It was probably the postman, seeing her car outside and wondering if she could take in a parcel for the neighbours.

She opened the door and stopped dead. 'You.'

'Yes, *cariña*. Me.'

In the weeks since she'd last seen Ramón he'd lost weight. There were distinct shadows under his eyes. And a shadow round his chin—although she normally disliked 'designer stubble', it made him look incredibly sexy.

Hormones, she told herself. You're immune to him, remember?

'Aren't you going to ask me in?'

'What do you want?'

He gave a mirthless laugh. 'I got your letter.'

'Oh?' She'd sent it weeks ago. Why hadn't he replied before?

Either her thoughts showed in her face or she'd spoken aloud, because his voice softened. 'You sent the letter to Sevilla. I've been away for a while.'

He didn't say where, she noticed.

'My post wasn't forwarded, so I only received it this morning.'

But if he'd only got it this morning, why was he here now?

'I got straight on the plane. I had to see you.' He frowned and stared at her. 'You look like hell.'

She lifted her chin. 'Hormones.'

'Ah, *cariña*.' To her shock, he reached out and caressed the slight swell of her stomach. 'Our baby.'

'Ramón…'

'I'm not going to discuss it on the doorstep. In fact,' he added, 'I'm not going to discuss it at all, Jennifer. There's only one thing we can do. You are going to marry me and give our child my name.'

He was going to marry her out of *duty*? 'Absolutely not.'

'No.' He shocked her further by picking her up and moving her bodily from the doorway. He set her down in the hallway and kicked the door shut behind him. 'We've played this your way for long enough. Now we'll do it my way. This afternoon we'll go into the city and apply for a marriage licence. Or if you'd prefer a church ceremony, we will talk to a vicar. I don't mind which. But you are going to marry me, Jennifer, make no mistake about that.'

'I think you're the one making a mistake,' she said softly. Dangerously softly. 'Because I'm not getting married to you or anyone else. I'm not letting anyone take over my life again.'

He stared at her as if she were mad. 'You're carrying my baby. *My* baby, Jennifer. Of course you're going to marry me.'

'I'm not trying to trap you into marriage,' she said. 'And I'm not going to let you trap me. I'm not going to be trapped again.'

He frowned. 'I'm obviously missing something, here. What do you mean, you're not going to be trapped again?'

'I've been there, done that, picked up the pieces—and it took me years. I'm not going to do it again.'

His frown deepened. 'But…your marriage…'

She gave a hollow laugh. 'Exactly.'

'I think,' Ramón said, 'it's time we talked.' His fingers circled her wrist. When she resisted, he tightened his grip just enough to tell her that he wasn't going to be put off by anything.

She let him lead her into the living room. He shepherded her to a chair. 'Sit down,' he said. 'I'll make us a drink. And then I think it's time you explained. *Everything*,' he emphasised.

CHAPTER ELEVEN

JENNIFER could hear Ramón moving easily round her kitchen, as if he'd lived there all his life. Well, he'd spent the best part of three months virtually living with her. Of course he knew his way around her kitchen. And she hadn't changed a thing since he'd gone.

'Would you like some herbal tea?' he called. 'Camomile's good.'

'Camomile's *revolting*,' she muttered. 'It's only there because it was a mixed pack and I've used up all the others.'

Ramón appeared in the doorway in time to see her grimace, and chuckled. 'You have a point. It might be good for you but it tastes vile. What would you like?'

'Just water, please.'

'Do you mind if I drink coffee?'

Even the thought of the smell was enough to make her gag. 'Yes.'

'OK. Do you need anything to eat?'

'Stop fussing. I'm pregnant, not ill,' she snapped.

He raised an eyebrow as if to add *And hormonal*, then went back to the kitchen. He returned with two glasses of water and sat next to her on the sofa. Too close for her comfort. But when she started to wriggle away, he grasped her wrist and kept her close. 'Now. Talk.' At her mutinous glare, he added, 'If we have to stay here all day and all night, you're going to tell me, Jennifer. No more secrets.'

'Says the man with the secret fiancée.'

'Sofía is *not* my…' He raked a hand through his hair in exasperation. 'You're trying to change the subject. All

138

right. I'll tell you the rest of it—the things I couldn't tell you before. *After* you explain to me about your husband.'

She was silent for a long, long time. Eventually, he stroked her cheek. '*Cariña*, it is better out than in. Tell me.'

She took a deep breath. 'I met Andrew when I was nearly eighteen. At an art exhibition. We were both studying the same picture and he started chatting to me. We went for a coffee afterwards, and…it just snowballed from there. He proposed to me three weeks later.' At the time, she'd been amazed, full of wonder that someone actually wanted her— wanted her enough to make her part of a family. 'It didn't seem to matter that he was a lot older than me. I was in love with him and I thought he loved me.' How wrong she'd been. Or maybe her definition of love had been different. 'We got married the day after my eighteenth birthday. Just before my exam results came back.' She swallowed. 'He persuaded me that I didn't need to study any more. I didn't need to work because I was his wife and he could support me. So I gave up my place at art college and settled down to being Mrs Jacobs.'

Ramón said nothing, but he was holding her hand and his thumb rubbed the back of her fingers in encouragement and sympathy.

'He didn't really like my friends—I think he felt a bit out of it because he was so much older than me—so I used to meet up with them during the day. But when they went to college, I lost touch with them. I did think maybe we could start a family, but he wasn't keen.'

'He didn't like children?'

'It wasn't that.' She took a deep breath. 'I didn't know who my parents were so we had no way of knowing if there was anything funny in my genes.'

'Funny?' Ramón queried, his voice very soft.

'I could be a carrier for something. Huntingdon's. Cystic

fibrosis. There are a dozen different diseases that...' Her voice cracked.

'Jennifer, *mi amor*. Listen to me. Our baby is going to be fine. Yes, there may be a risk that you're a carrier of something, but it is a tiny, tiny, tiny risk. And you know as well as I do that if only one parent is a carrier, the risks are even lower. There's no history of anything like that in my family.' His fingers tightened round hers. '*No te preocupes*. Everything will be fine.'

She couldn't share his confidence. And she couldn't tell him about the amnio. He'd feel obliged to stay with her if he knew, and she couldn't bear his pity.

'Jennifer? So what happened then? Your husband wouldn't let you work, wouldn't let you study, didn't like your friends.' He left the words unspoken but they both knew he was thinking it. *He wouldn't let you have a baby.*

'It didn't matter.' She shrugged. 'Andrew became my world. And then he had a heart attack at work when I was twenty-two. I didn't even get the chance to say goodbye to him—he was dead on arrival at the hospital. Without him...there was nothing left in my life. No job, no family, nothing. I thought about maybe reapplying to art college, but I'd missed my chance—and anyway, as Andrew said, I didn't really have what it took to make a real success of it. It would have been a waste of a place that someone else could have used, someone with real talent.'

She bit her lip. 'I ended up on antidepressants. But my GP was very good. She suggested counselling and after that getting a job where I could help people, something to give me a bit of purpose. So I started working as an auxiliary nurse. I was offered a place on the children's ward—and even though I knew I couldn't have children of my own...' She couldn't quite bring herself to say it, but nursing other people's children back to health had been the next best thing. 'I'd been there a couple of months when the sister asked me to go into her office. She said I was a natural and talked me into doing a nursing course. I wasn't sure if I was good enough, but I passed the exams and I've worked there ever since.'

Ramón was silent for a long, long time. She felt panic flooding through her. She'd spent years convincing herself that maybe Andrew had been wrong...but did Ramón feel the same way as Andrew? Had Andrew been right after all?

'I didn't expect *this*,' Ramón said eventually. 'You never spoke about your husband, there are no pictures of him... I thought it was because you loved him so much and couldn't bear the memories of what you had lost. That you were still mourning him, so many years later.'

'I was, in a way,' she said softly. 'I mourned the man I thought I'd married.'

'You still wear your wedding ring.' He rubbed his thumb against the gold band.

'As a reminder.' She pulled her hand from his. 'Something else I didn't tell you. Andrew was half-Spanish.'

Ramón's eyes widened.

'And I'm not going to fall into the same trap again.'

He exhaled sharply. 'I'm Spanish, too, but I'm not the same as your Andrew.'

She knew that. For a start, Andrew would have demanded immediately that she have a termination. But, she suddenly realized, she'd associated Ramón with the unhappiness she'd experienced with Andrew. She hadn't really given him a chance.

I would never stop you seeing your friends, stop you doing what you love, demand you do whatever I tell you.'

'No? Since the moment I opened the door, you've been bossing me about.'

'Because you exasperate me. I'm angry with you, Jennifer. Very angry.'

'I'm not the one who lied about being free.'

He said nothing. What could he say? It was the truth and they both knew it. She lifted her chin. 'I'm not going to let you bulldoze me into doing what you want, Ramón.'

'I'm not trying to bulldoze you. Well, maybe I am, a little,' he conceded, 'but I can't—'

He was cut off by the phone shrilling. 'Are you going to answer that?' he asked.

She shook her head—and then regretted it when there was a beep and Jill's voice floated into the room. 'JJ, it's Jill. I've booked you in for the amnio at ten o'clock tomorrow morning. Look, I know you said you wanted to do it on your own, but I'm not happy about it. I can pick you up at half past nine if you like—it's my day off so you're not taking me away from patients, and I didn't have anything planned so you're not imposing. I'm just worried about you. So give me a ring on my mobile when you get in, OK?'

Ramón was very, very still. 'Amnio?' he asked softly. 'Why are you having an amniocentesis, *cariña*?'

'Um…' There was no way she could back out of telling him now. As a qualified doctor, he'd be able to guess the answers. 'I was positive for the triple test,' she muttered.

'I'd managed to work that out for myself,' he said dryly. 'Which part?'

'Spina bifida.'

'Were you going to tell me?'

'Look, it's not important.'

He shook his head in exasperation. 'Yes, it is. This is my baby too.' He paused. 'Have you…made a decision?'

She nodded. 'I'm keeping the baby, regardless. This is just so I know the truth, so I can prepare myself for the worst if need be. But I'm not expecting you to stick around.'

'You think I'd desert you? Do you think I'm that dishonourable?'

'No.' But she couldn't bear him to stay out of pity and a sense of honour. She lifted her chin. 'I just don't want you around.'

He laughed shortly. 'I can disprove that in thirty seconds. All I have to do is carry you up the stairs to your bedroom.'

Her face flamed. 'How dare you?'

'Because it's true. The way you respond to me is the same as the way I respond to you. Look around you, Jennifer. I've kissed you on every chair in this room. I've made love to you in your garden, your bed, your shower... Every room in this house holds a memory for me. We were good together. And you want me to be around, Jennifer, every bit as much as I want to be here.'

'I am *not* going to put up with an Alpha male again,' she said though clenched teeth.

'Jennifer, I'm not going to boss you around.'

She scoffed. 'Like hell. It's all you've tried to do since you walked in.'

'All right. Then, yes, I am going to boss you around about some things. For the sake of our baby. I want you to ring Jill and tell her that there is no need to take you to the amnio. I'll take you myself.'

'There's no need.'

'Oh, yes, there is,' he said grimly. 'This is my baby too,' he repeated. 'And I'm going to support you through this difficult time, Jennifer, whether you like it or not.' He looked at her. 'Ring her.'

'No.'

'Then I'll do it for you.' He grabbed the phone, stood up, punched in the code to recall the last number dialled, then pressed the button to call Jill back.

'Hello? Is that Jill?' He ignored Jennifer's glare. 'No, you haven't spoken to me before. My name is Ramón Martínez. I'm calling on behalf of Jennifer. Yes, *that* Jennifer.' He smiled thinly. 'Thank you for your offer to take her to the amnio, but it is OK. I will do it. Yes. Yes, I am.' His smile broadened. 'Oh, yes,' he said emphatically. 'You can count on that.'

'What did you just say to her?' Jennifer asked through gritted teeth when he cut the connection and replaced the phone.

'I answered her questions.'

'Which were?'

'What do you think?'

Whether he was the father of her baby—and whether he was going to stand by her. She'd bet her last penny on that. She scowled. 'Why do you always answer a question with a question?'

He laughed. 'Why do you?'

'I hate you, Ramón.'

'No. You're angry with me. Just as I'm angry with you. But we will work through it, *mi amor*.'

'Maybe I don't want to.'

'Maybe you have no choice.' Still standing, he folded his arms and stared at her. 'You're having an amniocentesis tomorrow. That means you will need to rest for a couple of days. So have you called in sick, or were you planning to take annual leave?'

'I...I hadn't really thought that far ahead,' Jennifer admitted. 'I'm off tomorrow anyway.'

'Have you told anyone at work that you are pregnant?'

'Um—not yet.'

'You must be, what, seventeen weeks?'

'How do you know?'

'Because the triple test is done at fifteen weeks and the results take ten days or so. It doesn't take a mathematical genius to work it out.'

She flushed. 'No.'

He sighed. '*Lo siente*. I'm sorry for snapping. But you take self-reliance to such extremes. It infuriates me.

Jennifer, the hospital needs to know that you are pregnant. They need to prepare for maternity cover. And you have rights too. Time off for antenatal appointments and the right to stay away from anything dangerous for the baby, such as X-rays.'

'Oh, so you're not decreeing that I have to stay at home with the baby after it's born?'

'Of course not. You love your job. And until the baby arrives, you won't know whether you want to stay at home or go back to work full time or work out some kind of compromise,' he said. 'But even you must admit that you'll need a little time off after the birth.'

Her throat ached with unshed tears. 'I can support myself. I don't need you.'

'Tough. You're stuck with me. You have no other family to look after you. The baby is mine, so that makes *me* your family.' He gave her an uncompromising stare. 'And I'm going to look after you.'

She stared at him in disbelief. 'Are you saying *you're* giving up work?'

'For the moment, yes.'

'Isn't that a bit extreme? I mean, don't you have to work out a notice period or something?'

'No.'

How could Ramón take an unspecified amount of time off work? Financially, she assumed that he had enough family money to keep him going if he wanted to take a sabbatical. But workwise...he must be very senior indeed, she thought, for his hospital to let him have as much time off as he wanted. And he couldn't be more than thirty-five. 'And you say I keep things to myself,' she muttered.

'You do. Why didn't you tell me about Andrew before?'

'Because...' Because she'd wanted to try to forget it. Because she hadn't wanted Ramón to pity her. Because she hadn't wanted Ramón to despise her. And a hundred and one other reasons.

'OK. I won't bully you about Andrew. But I *will* bully you about the amnio. Now, you know what the procedure is?'

She rolled her eyes. 'Of course I do. I'm a qualified nurse.'

'In paediatrics, not obstetrics.'

'And you did a stint in obstetrics, did you?' she asked nastily.

'As a matter of fact, yes.' He sighed. 'Jennifer, you're being difficult.'

'I'm not.'

'Yes, you are.' He sat down next to her on the sofa again and, before she realised what he was going to do he pulled her onto his lap.

She knew she should pull away. For her own sanity. But it felt so good to be in his arms again. So good to be held, to be cherished. She'd missed him. Missed the sound of his heartbeat, the feel of his skin against hers, his warm, clean male scent. She couldn't help sinking back against him, resting her head on his shoulder, letting him support her. He settled her more comfortably against him and clasped his hands together round her waist. 'Now, *cariña*, the amnio. They'll do an ultrasound so they can see where the baby is and the safest place to put the needle into the amniotic fluid around the baby. They'll take twenty millilitres or so of fluid—that's about four teaspoons—and then they'll culture the cells to see what is going on with the baby. It won't hurt the baby and you should feel nothing more than you would for any routine vaccination, just a tiny scratch. But there is a risk of miscarriage. A small risk, but it's important that you rest afterwards to minimise that risk.'

'Jill told me they don't insist on bed rest afterwards now-adays.'

'Let us be very clear about this, *cariña*. This is our baby and you're not going to take any risks. For the next three days, you're staying put. Preferably in bed, but I will allow you to sit on the sofa or in a chair, provided you rest. You are certainly not going to work.'

'You will *allow* me to sit,' she said through clenched teeth, incensed by his high-handedness.

'I know I'm bossing you about and you hate it. But that's only because I can't wrap you in cotton wool—because I can't have the amnio in your place and take the pain and worry away from you,' he said, shocking her. 'Now, during these three days, I'll try very hard to be tidy. But I'm afraid we will be living on take-away food or cold meals, because my cooking is not up to your standards.'

'Hang on. You're telling me that you're moving in?'

'Yes.'

'Just for a couple of days. Until I'm over the amnio.'

Ramón shrugged.

Meaning what? That he intended to stay permanently? She panicked. 'I don't want you to move in.'

'What other choice do you have?'

She scowled. 'I hate you.'

He kissed the top of her head. 'Do you, now?'

Her eyes filled with tears. 'I hate you.'

'I hated you,' he said. 'When I was at the airport. When they'd called my flight three times and I still couldn't see you. When I had to walk onto that plane, knowing that you didn't love me enough to see me before I went.'

How wrong he was. But he hadn't loved her enough to tell her the truth. 'You said there was something else about Sofía.'

He nodded. 'I couldn't tell you at the time, because it wasn't my secret to tell.'

Jennifer stiffened. 'Are you still engaged to her?'

'No. And I told you before, I was never in love with her and she was never in love with me. She's always been more like my sister than anything else. Even when I was a hormonally charged teenager, I don't think I even kissed her.' He rubbed his cheek against her hair. 'Whereas I wanted to kiss you the minute I saw you.'

And she wanted him to kiss her, too. Right now. It would be so, so easy to reach up to him—but she needed to know the truth first.

'Anyway, my parents expected me to take a business degree and join the family business, but that's not where my heart lay. Sofía encouraged me to follow my dreams to go to med school while she went to some finishing school or other. And while she was there, she had an...unsuitable liaison, in her parents' view. She fell in love with someone who wasn't of the same class, someone who didn't have money and land and family connections. She knew her parents would never accept a marriage to Miguel. So she moved to Madrid. So did he. And they saw each other in secret.'

'So where does your engagement fit in?'

'If her parents thought she was engaged to me, they wouldn't question her about her life in Madrid—her job, her friends, who she was seeing—because of course as my *novia* she wouldn't be seeing another man.' He sighed. 'And it suited me, too. If my parents thought I was engaged to her, they would stop haranguing me about being a doctor or getting more medical experience in England because, of course, I'd come back to my *novia* and settle down. Though I promise you there was nothing romantic between us. I was just her cover for Miguel, and she was my cover for my job.'

'But what about your girlfriends? Didn't they mind?'

He shrugged. 'I was actually rather studious and concentrated on my work, not my love life. After my first couple of years as a student, before Sofía and I got engaged.' He gave her a wicked grin. 'I'm afraid I was like any other eighteen-year-old male. Rampaging hormones and all that.'

'Didn't Miguel mind that she was supposed to be engaged to you?'

'Yes,' Ramón said simply. 'He wanted to claim his woman in public. But Sofía didn't want her parents to disown her—which they would have done, had she married Miguel. This way, she kept everyone happy.' He nuzzled her cheek. 'What I didn't bargain for was you.'

'Does Sofía know?'

'About you? Yes. She was the first person I saw when I went back to Spain. But before I could tell her that I wanted to end our engagement and tell our families the truth, she told me that she was going to marry Miguel. You see, *querida*, you are not the only one expecting a *niño*.'

She stared at him in shock. 'Sofía is pregnant?'

'Six months. She looks round and disgustingly happy. And she is now Señora Corvela.' He grinned. 'I was the main witness at the wedding. And, of course, I am expected back in Madrid for the christening. Sofía does not believe in godparents by proxy.'

'So...'

'So I wasn't lying to you, *mi amor*. It really was a technical engagement—something to keep our families happy.'

'But surely they wanted you to set a wedding date?'

'The engagement was enough. A promise that we would settle down and do our parents' bidding one day.'

'Do they know now?'

'Oh, yes. I was the one who broke the news—while Miguel and Sofía were away on honeymoon.' A honeymoon that had been his wedding present to them, but Jennifer didn't need to know that.

'When I told Sofía's mother, I'm surprised you didn't

hear the fireworks here in England. But she secretly likes the idea of being *abuela*, a grandmother, having a *niño* to spoil. She's coming round to the idea. And, most importantly, she hasn't disowned her daughter.' He stroked Jennifer's hair. 'My own mother, although she would die rather than admit it, is jealous in the extreme at Carla being a grandmother when *she* isn't. So when she knows that we are having a baby, too…she will be pleased.'

'But what if…?' Jennifer whispered—then stopped.

Ramón knew instinctively what she was too scared to say aloud, in case she was tempting fate. '*Cariña*, she will love our baby, whatever. Because it's *our* baby,' he emphasised. 'But I think you are right to keep things quiet for now. Until we know. And we will tell the world when *we* are ready.'

CHAPTER TWELVE

'SO WHAT were you planning to do today?' Ramón asked, after he'd made them both a sandwich for lunch and made a huge fuss of Spider—who was ecstatic at seeing Ramón again and miaowed loudly and rubbed himself against Ramón's legs and then took up his old position curled round his shoulders.

'Painting.'

'Portraits of Spider?' he asked, scratching the cat between his ears.

Jennifer shook her head. 'Not that sort of painting. The nursery. I was putting the dust sheets down when you turned up.'

His lips thinned. 'You were going to climb ladders, despite the fact that you're pregnant?'

She rolled her eyes. 'I'm pregnant, not ill.'

'And if you'd slipped and fallen? You could have hurt the baby.'

The baby. Not her. Of course. The baby was his first concern. She was a poor second best. 'I wouldn't do anything stupid.'

'Too right. You stick to the bottom half. I'll do the top.'

She blinked. 'You're going to paint my nursery?'

'No. *We* are going to paint our baby's nursery. Together.'

'But...' That was the sort of thing that real partners did. And Ramón wasn't her partner any more.

'Jennifer, *querida*, I'm not totally useless.' He gave her a wry smile. 'I can just about manage to put paint on a wall without making it look a mess. What colour did you choose?'

'Yellow.'

'So our baby will wake up bathed in sunlight.'

She wished he'd stop doing this 'our' business. It reminded her too much of Andrew. How long would it be before 'our' changed to 'my'?

But, to her surprise, Ramón was easy to work with. He did his share of the room immaculately, and finished before she did—but he didn't try to take over from her. He simply made her a cup of hot chocolate and made sure she rested before she finished painting her section of the walls.

He cleaned the brushes—and then he brought his bag in from the car and took a shower. And for every second that the water ran, she remembered the time he'd made love to her in her shower. Worse, when he emerged from the bathroom, he was fully clothed but his hair was damp. It brought back even more memories. Memories of making love in his flat and then rushing back to the ward.

'Would you like pizza, Indian or Chinese?' he asked.

'Pizza sounds good.'

'Anything special on it?'

A wicked impulse seized her. 'If I said banana?'

'Then I'll order it for you, *querida*.' He raised an eyebrow. 'Now, are you teasing or are you serious?'

He really *would* order it for her. 'Teasing,' she said hastily.

After they'd eaten—pizza *without* an extra topping of banana—Ramón insisted on doing the washing-up while she rested. When he came back into the living room, bringing her a glass of water with a slice of lemon, she came to a decision.

'Would you like to see a picture?'

'Picture?'

'Of the baby. The scan.'

His eyes brightened. 'I'd love to.'

She took the square card frame from her handbag and passed it to him silently.

He stared at it, then traced the outline of the baby reverently with his forefinger. He didn't say a word but Jennifer could see his lips moving, as if he were talking to the picture. His face was filled with awe, and pride, and some other emotion she didn't dare name in case she was wrong.

'Thank you,' he said at last, handing the scan picture back to her. 'Thank you for showing me our *niño.*'

She felt guilty now for not having a copy she could give him to keep. But at the time she'd been completely on her own. She hadn't thought she'd ever see him again.

The awkward moment passed and they spent the rest of the evening listening to music. Though Ramón, she noticed, didn't sit with her again. He made a fuss of her cat, but kept away from her.

And then came the moment she was really dreading. Bedtime. 'You're sleeping on the sofa,' Jennifer warned him.

He shrugged. 'As you wish, *cariña.*'

He fetched spare bedding from her airing cupboard and made himself a bed on her sofa. Even though he was doing what she'd asked, she couldn't suppress unreasonable disappointment. He hadn't made even a token protest. So he couldn't still feel the same about her. She hadn't noticed a single flicker of passion in his eyes when he'd looked at her. Not when they'd shared the pizza, not even when she'd shown him the picture of their baby.

Because he was there out of duty. He saw her as the mother of his child, and that was the only reason he cosseted her. He didn't really want *her.* All that stuff earlier about wanting to hold her had been because he'd thought it was what she wanted to hear. He hadn't meant it, deep down. It had just been lip service.

Now he was here, she realised what she really wanted. A family of her own. A family who loved her. Ramón would marry her tomorrow for the baby's sake, but that wasn't what she wanted—she wanted to be loved for herself, not for the baby's sake. Was that why her mother had split up with her father, because she too hadn't wanted to be second best? And this, this travesty of a relationship, after what they'd shared before... She didn't want this. She didn't want his pity.

Jennifer lay awake for a long, long time. However much she plumped her pillow, she couldn't get comfortable. And although she told herself she was just nervous about tomorrow, she knew the real reason why she couldn't sleep. Because Ramón was downstairs. And he might just as well be a million miles away.

Some time later she heard a creak, and then her bedroom door opened.

'*Cariña*, it's me,' he said softly.

'What do you want?'

He sighed and came to sit on the edge of her bed. 'Your sofa is uncomfortable. And...' He sighed again. 'No. Your sofa isn't that bad. I've slept in worse places. But I can't stay down there, knowing that you're lying here with our baby inside you.' He reached for her hand and drew it to his lips. 'I will make no demands of you, Jennifer. I don't expect you to make love with me. But I want to hold you tonight, sleep with you in my arms.'

As the mother of his child. Not his lover.

'Please?'

There was a raw note in his voice which stopped her telling him to leave. She simply turned on her side and shifted over slightly, and Ramón slid under the duvet next to her. He moved to lie against her, spoon-style, and curved one arm round her waist. As if he were holding the baby, she thought, not her.

She was intensely aware that Ramón was wearing absolutely nothing. He never had worn anything in bed in all the time she'd known him. And her cotton nightie was little barrier between them. She was aware of the warmth of his body, the sprinkling of hairs on his chest.

And she was very aware of the fact that Ramón wasn't aroused.

So it really, really *wasn't* her he wanted to hold, she thought. It was the baby that had brought him to her. Not because he'd missed *her*, whatever he claimed. She forced her breathing to become deep and regular. At least if he thought she was asleep, he wouldn't try to have a conversation with her. But she wasn't prepared for him to start talking to the baby. In whispered Spanish, his voice low and intense. She had no idea what he was saying—and no way was she going to ask for a translation.

A tear leaked over the bridge of her nose and soaked into her pillow. She forced herself to stay rigidly still, not wanting Ramón to know she was crying. But just when she'd thought she couldn't possibly hurt any more, she discovered that she could. And did.

The next morning, Jennifer woke with a headache. And a sense of relief that Ramón was already awake and out of bed. She hoped he was dressed. She really didn't want to face him when he was naked.

The bedroom door opened abruptly and she pulled the duvet over her to cover herself as Ramón walked in, fully dressed.

A flicker of annoyance crossed his face at her action. 'I'm perfectly capable of controlling myself, you know.'

'Sorry.'

'And I'm not going to stand here holding this all day, so can you sit up?'

She did, and he placed the tray on her lap. 'Toast, cold

water with a slice of lemon. Is there anything else you'd like?'

He'd made her breakfast. And there was a flower on the tray. Her eyes pricked with tears. 'I'm sorry.'

'So am I.' He sat on the edge of the bed and held her hand. 'You know why we're snapping at each other. We're both worried, both want our baby to be all right. But I rang the clinic this morning—the doctor who's seeing us is the most experienced one in the hospital.'

'You rang the clinic?' she said, surprised.

'Yes.' He rubbed his hand across his eyes. 'I got their answering-machine twice. Then the cleaner. Then I realised it was only seven o'clock and I'd convinced myself it was already eight.'

So he was as nervous as she was...

'Take your time over breakfast, *cariña*. We have plenty of time.'

Time to worry. Time to get worked up.

'Oh—and there'll be another glass of water to follow that one. You need to drink a lot to make sure there's a good ultrasound picture.'

'I know.'

'Call me if you need me.' He squeezed her hand and left the room.

She wasn't going to cry. She really wasn't. But the toast tasted like ashes in her mouth, and it was an effort to force the water down. She showered and washed her hair, then dressed slowly and went downstairs to join Ramón. He was reading the paper as if he didn't have a care in the world, sitting on the sofa with Spider curled round his shoulders.

He looked up. 'Ready for your next glass of water?'

'If I have to.'

'I know it's uncomfortable, having a full bladder with a baby pressing on it, but if you don't do it here you'll have to do it in the clinic.' He gently lifted Spider off his shoulders and the cat miaowed in protest. 'Hey, *gatito*, I think someone around here needs a cuddle from you,' he said softly.

Two seconds later Spider wound himself round her legs. She sat down and made a fuss of the cat, then glanced up at the clock. There was so long still to wait. And what if the clinic was running late?

To her relief, when they reached the hospital, the clinic was running absolutely on time. She didn't have the extra torture of waiting.

'Mrs Jacobs?'

They stood up together and Ramón held Jennifer's hand tightly. He kept holding her hand all the way into the ultrasound room and all the while that the sonographer was smearing the radioconductive gel onto her abdomen and the obstetrician was explaining the procedure. And when the picture came up on the screen and they could both see the baby there, sucking its thumb and lying contentedly on its back with its legs crossed, she saw wonder cross his face.

'Our baby,' he said, his voice thick with emotion. 'I missed the first scan,' he explained to the sonographer. 'Look, *querida*—a perfect heartbeat.'

Was it her imagination, or was there a film of tears in his eyes?

She gripped his hand as the needle went in. He rubbed his thumb against her skin. 'Be brave, *cariña*,' he whispered. '*Tranquilo, no pasa nada.*'

'All done,' the obstetrician said with a smile. 'Two weeks, and we'll know what's going on. Though if it helps, I can't see anything that concerns me on the scan.'

'It helps,' Ramón said softly. 'Thank you.'

'We'll ring you with the results. Though if there should be anything to worry about, your GP will call you instead and talk things through with you,' she said. She handed them a piece of paper. 'If you haven't heard in a fortnight, ring the number at the top.'

'If I haven't heard...?' Jennifer questioned.

'Very, very occasionally the culture doesn't take.'

'So we'd have to go through all this again?' she asked.

Ramón squeezed her hand. 'It's a very, very tiny chance, *cariña*.'

'Very tiny,' the obsetrician agreed. 'But you need to be prepared, so if it does happen it won't be such a shock. Now, Mrs Jacobs, you need to take it easy for the next day or so.'

'She will.'

Jennifer glared at Ramón as she wiped the gel from her stomach. 'I can speak for myself.'

'Yes, and if I let you have your way you'll be hanging curtains or be up a ladder cleaning the windows.' When she'd restored order to her clothes, he helped her to her feet. 'It's a girl,' he said with a grin. 'Definitely. As stubborn as her *madre*.'

'We can tell you the baby's sex, if you'd like to know,' the obstetrician said.

'No, thanks. I'd like it to stay a surprise,' Jennifer said.

Ramón slid his arm round her shoulders. 'Your call, *cariña*.'

At least he wasn't going to argue, Jennifer thought.

He drove her home extremely slowly and extremely carefully. She could feel her temper rising. If he wrapped her in cotton wool, she'd go bananas. She just wanted to get back to work and forget about the two-week wait.

But Ramón did exactly what she feared. He was inexorable. 'Bed,' he said when she unlocked the door to her cottage. 'And you do not get up until this evening at the very earliest. Understood?'

'Ramón—'

'*Bed.* I will bring you a drink, a sandwich and something to read.'

To her surprise, he brought her a pile of baby magazines.

'Where did you get these?' she asked.

'The newsagent.' He sighed. 'I couldn't sleep and I didn't want to disturb you, so I went for a walk this morning before I rang the clinic.'

And bought every single baby magazine on the shelves. She didn't have the heart to tell him she'd already read half of them. 'Thanks.'

'So. Show me what sort of thing you'd like for the nursery.'

Her eyes narrowed. 'Why?'

'It will give you something to think about,' he said softly. 'And while away a few minutes.'

He sat on the bed next to her, leafing through the magazines, and encouraged her to point out furniture and curtains and a comfortable nursing chair. And then he took the magazines from her. 'Time for a *siesta*,' he said.

'I'm not tired.'

'*Cariña*, it has been a tough morning. And strain makes you tired. Try to have a nap,' he said.

'I'm really not tired.'

'I'll lie here with you for a little while,' he said. He closed the curtains, then came back to the bed and lay down beside her. On top of the duvet, she noticed. So he didn't want to be *that* close to her. He slid his arm round her and fitted his body into the curve of her own, then pressed a kiss to her hair. 'Now, close your eyes,' he said. 'Imagine you're lying back and watching the sky. It's blue, very blue, and there are white fluffy clouds floating over it. And now you're in the cloud. You're sitting in the cloud. It's cool and soft and so comfortable. And you're so tired. You lean back and close your eyes and relax, knowing the cloud will support you and soothe you. And then...'

Even though part of her mind was fighting it, and wanted to know just where Ramón had learned relaxation exercises and why he was so good at it, she found her eyes growing heavy and she drifted into sleep, thinking of the cloud and feeling somehow secure in Ramón's arms.

She woke to find herself alone. She could hear Ramón talking downstairs and frowned. Did they have visitors? Or was he on the phone? She stretched. Whatever. She'd had enough of staying in bed like an invalid. She got up, pulled her dressing gown on and padded downstairs in bare feet.

'What are you doing up?' Ramón asked.

'I woke up. Who were you talking to?'

'No one important.' He spoke lightly, but he looked guilty. Or was she overreacting? 'Would you like anything to eat?'

'Not yet.'

'Then go back to bed, *cariña*,' he ordered.

'Ramón, I'll go crazy if you make me stay in bed all the time.'

He sighed. 'All right. You can stay up. But you sit on the sofa with your feet up and you don't move.' Her frustration must have shown in her face, because he added, 'Come on. We'll watch a film. I'll make us some popcorn.'

It was revolting. Burned. But at least he'd tried. And he was so solicitous, making sure she was comfortable on the sofa, bring her an extra cushion to support her back, giving her a footrub.

If only he was doing it because he loved her, and not because she was carrying his child and he saw it as his duty.

The next day was more of the same—Ramón refusing to let her get up until lunchtime, waiting on her hand and foot, and in the meantime working in her dining room. She'd seen files and a laptop when she'd peeked round the door, but hadn't quite had the nerve to go in and ask what he was doing.

But eventually she cracked. 'It's worse for me, being in bed. I've got nothing to do except lie there and think.'

'Think the worst. And worry.' He exhaled sharply. 'All right. You can sit in a chair and talk to me while I paint the woodwork in the nursery. But stay in the doorway—even with the windows open, there will be fumes and they're not good for you or the baby.'

She chatted to him about everything and nothing while she watched him work. He was methodical but fast, and the results were perfect. He'd stripped down to just a pair of cut-off denims while he worked, and she was uncomfortably aware of how attractive he was. Her mouth went dry as she watched the play of muscles in his back as he painted a corner. She wanted him. Wanted him badly.

But there was no point in doing anything about it, because she knew he didn't want her.

On the third day of resting, she was irritable and found fault with everything.

'OK. I can take a hint. You can go back to work tomorrow,' Ramón said. 'On condition that I take you to work and pick you up after your shift.'

She curled her lip. 'That's the sort of thing Andrew would have said.'

He folded his arms. '*Cariña*, I'm not Andrew. I'm not trying to keep you from your work and your friends—I just want to be sure that you don't overdo things and make yourself ill. I'm not going to be waiting in the car park, tapping my fingers on the steering-wheel because you're a minute late.'

How had he guessed Andrew had always done that?

'If you want to go out with your friends after work, that's fine. Just ring my mobile twenty minutes before you want me to pick you up, tell me where to meet you and I'll be there.'

'All right.' She knew she was being ungracious, but she really couldn't help it. 'Ramón, I'm not going to tell people at work about the baby until the results come back.'

'Your colleagues, yes, but I think you should tell the clinical director. Pete's a nice guy. He'll keep it confidential but he'll also look after you.'

Something in his tone alerted her. 'You've already told him, haven't you?'

'It…came up in conversation,' Ramón said carefully.

'Why are you interfering?'

'Because it's my baby, too.'

Of course. The baby. Her heart sank. He was worried about his potential son and heir, not the mother of his child.

He dropped her off at the hospital the next morning. 'What are your plans for today?' she asked.

'A bit of work, play with Spider, this and that. And I'll try not to make too much of a mess,' he said. 'Ring my mobile when you want me to pick you up.'

If he was going back to the cottage, why didn't he want her to ring him there? Unless… No. She wasn't going to start speculating. It didn't matter anyway because they didn't have a future and he didn't want her. 'See you later,' she muttered.

He didn't even kiss her goodbye. And she was thoroughly out of sorts by the time she walked onto the ward. She reassured Meg that she was over her 'stomach bug'—thank heaven she wasn't showing much yet, and could claim that her thickened waist was merely because she'd been eating too any chocolates—and went to check on her first patient, a little girl who'd been admitted with a severe asthma attack, made worse by the fact that her parents smoked and hadn't been giving her the prevention inhaler properly.

By the time Ramón picked her up, Jennifer had recovered her equanimity. And the next day she managed to throw herself completely into work, to the point where she could blank out the fact that she was waiting for the test results.

And then she saw him when she was coming back from her coffee-break. He had his back to her and was talking to a group of doctors. Her heart stopped. No. It couldn't be anything to do with the test results. No matter how many strings he pulled, he couldn't make the cells grow any faster. They had to wait for nine more days. And the hospital would have contacted her first anyway.

So what was going on?

When she rang him to let him know she was nearly ready to meet him that evening, she couldn't help saying. 'I saw you at the hospital today.'

'I was bored. Dropped in to see some old friends,' he said. 'I was thinking about coming up to the ward, asking if you wanted to have lunch with me—but I didn't want you to think that I was being a control freak and checking up on you.'

Well, she deserved that.

'And people would have talked. Gossiped about why I was meeting you.'

'Right.' She knew she deserved that, too.

'I'll see you in the car park when you're ready, then,' he told her.

'Thanks.' And as she cut the connection, her frown deepened. Either she was imagining things or she'd heard a woman's voice. Low and laughing and husky. A woman, talking to Ramón.

So that was why he'd told her to call his mobile. Because he wasn't at the cottage—he was somewhere else. With another woman. Pain seared its way through her. She had no idea how long the affair had been going on. But then again, it wasn't her business any more, because there was only one reason why he was even staying at the cottage.

The baby.

And that wasn't enough. Tonight, she'd tell him. She'd tell him he could have access to the baby whenever he wanted, but she didn't want him in the cottage any more. She could cope perfectly well on her own.

CHAPTER THIRTEEN

IN THE end, Jennifer chickened out of tackling him. Ramón didn't seem to notice that she was silent or angry when he met her after work. He just chatted casually to her on the way home as if nothing was wrong. He made them a salad and served it with cold chicken he'd bought from the deli and some jacket potatoes, then urged her to put her feet up and read a magazine while he did some work.

She knew he was writing some paper or other—she'd managed to get that much out of him—but he hadn't discussed it with her. Part of her felt vaguely hurt. Whatever their personal differences, she knew he respected her professionally. She could have helped him.

Clearly he didn't want her help. Didn't want her, full stop. The only time he laid a hand on her was in bed at night, and even then she knew he was holding the bump, not her.

Eight days. Eight more days and they'd know. The closer the deadline for the test results loomed, the slower time seemed to go. Dragging by. She'd look at her watch, expecting half an hour to have gone by, and it had been less than five minutes.

When Ramón met her after her late shift that evening, he seemed particularly pleased with himself. 'So what's the big secret?' she asked, aware that she sounded peevish and snappy but completely unable to stop herself.

'*Mañana*,' he said.

'What are you up to?' she demanded.

'Nothing for you to worry about, *cariña*,' he said. 'Now, have you eaten properly tonight?'

She groaned. 'Don't start that cotton-wool stuff again.'

'Fair enough.'

How could he be so calm when she was being so unreasonable? She brooded all the way home. And all the way through the warm-but-not-too-warm-because-it's-bad-for-the-baby bath he ran for her. And later that evening when she went to bed and turned her back on him.

But then, as his hand curved round her abdomen, she felt it. A distinct pulsing movement. Right under his hand.

He went very, very still. '*Querida?* Did you...did you feel that?' he whispered.

'Yes,' she whispered back.

'Our baby just kicked. To say hello,' he whispered, stroking her stomach.

The baby kicked again.

'*Hola, mi niño,*' he whispered. 'Hello, my baby.'

She tried desperately not to cry, but her shudder was enough to make him draw her closer. '*Querida*, don't worry. *Tranquilo*. Everything will be fine,' he said. His voice was just as shaky as hers. She curled her fingers round his, needing the comfort. He held her close, saying nothing but letting the warmth of his body take the chill and the fear from hers.

And as she drifted to sleep, she was sure she felt the lightest possible touch of his lips against her shoulder.

Or maybe she was dreaming. Wishing. Hoping for something that could never happen again.

Jennifer was on a late the next day. Again, Ramón brought her breakfast in bed, along with the morning paper, and refused to let her get up.

'You're working until eight tonight, so you'll be

tired when you get home,' he said. 'Grab some rest while you can.'

He seemed in a hurry to get her out of the house, but she made no protest. If she asked no questions, he could tell her no lies.

Seven days to go, she thought as she walked into the hospital. It was almost midday. If she heard first thing, that still meant one hundred and sixty-five hours to wait. Nine thousand, nine hundred minutes. Over half a million seconds. How could she bear it?

Worse still was her first case that morning, a new patient with Klippel-Feil syndrome, a condition that often went with spina bifida. A condition that maybe her own child could have.

Please, no, she prayed silently outside the ward. Please, don't let this happen to my baby, too. And although she was her usual calm, collected self on the outside, inside she was panicking. The voice in her head was growing louder and louder. *What if? What if?*

That evening, when she got into the car, she turned to Ramón. 'What do you know about Klippel-Feil syndrome?' she asked.

Ramón raised an eyebrow. 'Giving me a viva, *querida*?' At her rolled eyes, he smiled ruefully. 'Sorry. Do you have a patient with it?'

Jennifer nodded.

'OK. It's a congenital fusion of at least two of the vertebrae in the cervical part of the spine—the defect occurs somewhere between the fifth and eighth week of gestation. It's more common in girls, and we're not sure how common it is because if it's very mild it might not even be diagnosed. Sufferers usually have a short neck, a low hairline at the back and they can't move their necks as much as someone without the condition. Depending on how the spine is affected, he or she is more likely to have neuro-

logical problems after a minor trauma. There may be a need
for surgery to make sure there's no instability in the neck
or skull, or if the spinal canal is narrowed to relieve con-
striction of the spinal cord. But generally patients who
aren't severely affected can lead perfectly normal lives.
They just need to avoid any activities that could injure the
neck.'

She took a deep breath. 'There are other conditions that
go with it, aren't there?'

'Yes. Scoliosis is the most common one, and then—' He
stopped abruptly before mentioning the words she expected
next. *Spina bifida.* '*Cariña*, you've already done some research on this, haven't you?'

She nodded.

He reached his left hand across to her and patted hers.
'We don't know that our baby definitely has spina bifida.
And Klippel-Feil is something else entirely.'

'But it's genetic.'

'There's some research going on to find out if there is a
gene responsible. There are a lot of non-genetic cases as
well,' he said.

'But there's a genetic component.' She clenched her
hands so hard that her knuckles were white. Why didn't he
understand? 'And I don't know if it's in my family.'

'It doesn't *matter*,' he said emphatically. '*Querida*, I
know you're worried. But the chances are that there are no
genetic disorders of any kind in your family.' He patted
her hand again.

She was too choked to say anything. Hormones, she kept
telling herself. It was just her hormones going into over-
drive and making her moody. But inside she was panicking.
What if? What if?

When they got back to the cottage, Ramón stood at the
foot of the stairs. 'There's something I want to talk to you
about.'

Oh, lord. Here it came. He was going to tell her about the woman he'd been talking to. That he'd fallen in love. That—

'Jennifer?'

'Sorry. I missed that.'

'You're drifting off, because you're overdoing things.' He sighed. 'In five minutes' time you're going to rest, whether you like it or not. But before you do—come with me.'

He led her up the stairs. Jennifer was shivering inside. What was he going to tell her?

He stopped outside the closed door of nursery. 'Close your eyes.'

She frowned. 'What?'

'Close your eyes,' he repeated. Then added, 'Humour me?'

The one phrase she couldn't resist. She closed her eyes.

'OK. You can open them now,' he said softly.

She did. And gasped in amazement when she saw what he'd done. The room they'd painted together was completely transformed. There was a beech cot in the corner of the room—the one she'd picked out of the magazine—together with a matching changing station and a comfortable nursing chair. The curtains were green and covered with zoo animals, and a large felt caterpillar hanging snaked across the wall, each pocket filled with a finger-puppet of an animal for each letter of the alphabet. The ceiling had been painted a pale blue and fluffy clouds danced across it, with a sun in one corner and a wide rainbow. Butterflies hung off one mobile, bluebirds on another.

'Ramón... You did this?'

'Er, not all of it,' he admitted. 'A friend of a friend in London is a nursery designer. I told her what we wanted and she did the arty bits for me while I did the shopping.

They're her mobiles, too. And the clock. And the caterpillar was designed by another of her friends.'

The clock was in the shape of a black and white dog, with large numbers painted in red and blue hands.

She did the arty bits for me. So that was the husky-voiced woman he'd been talking to. And why he'd been so shifty about what he'd been doing—he'd planned this as a surprise for her.

He wasn't having an affair.

How stupid she'd been. Hormonal, fretting over nothing. Of course he hadn't been having an affair. Her heart soared and she felt as if it would burst from her.

'This was the furniture you liked, wasn't it?' he asked, sounding a little less assured than normal.

She nodded, unable to speak.

'I know I should have told you first. Asked you. But I wanted to surprise you…to make you smile.' He walked into the room and took the bear from the cot. 'I hope you don't mind, but I wanted to buy our baby's first teddy. I had one like this when I was a child.'

A Steiff bear, she noted absently. Very expensive. And utterly beautiful.

'Jennifer? *Querida*, don't cry. I can paint it all out again, send the furniture back if you don't like it.' He folded her in his arms with a muffled exclamation. 'Hey. It's all right. *No te preoccupes.*'

But it wasn't all right, she thought. He was holding her now, but tenderly, with kindness. As he would have held anybody who was crying. She realised now he wasn't having an affair, but that didn't mean he still loved her. Since he'd been back he'd barely touched her. He hadn't kissed her—not properly anyway. This really wasn't going to work. It *wasn't* going to be all right. And she was deluding herself if she listened to him.

*   *   *

Six days. Five.

The countdown slowed. Four. Three.

Two. Jennifer took to watching the clock. Constantly. Willing the hands to move faster, let her know the truth at last.

And on the day she'd been waiting for, longing for and dreading in equal measures, she was off duty. Ramón was in a meeting at Brad's, something to do with the paper he was writing. He could have changed it, she thought bitterly, but no. Obviously he'd forgotten what day it was. A wave of nausea spilled over her. He'd forgotten because he didn't care enough. He'd just told her to call him on his mobile if she needed him—and they both knew that his mobile would be diverted to voicemail, switched off in the hospital itself.

She couldn't settle to anything. Watched the clock, seeing the seconds tick by, the hands moving painfully round the dial. Nine o'clock, and nothing. Her fingers began to tingle with adrenalin. Half-past nine, and still nothing. Maybe the cells hadn't cultured properly and she'd have to go through all this again. Ten o'clock, and still no call. Maybe there was a backlog. A fire alarm. Someone off sick. Half past ten, and she went to get her gardening gloves. At least if she was busy weeding, she wouldn't sit there watching the clock and getting more and more upset and desperate to know what the delay was. Wouldn't be convincing herself that the delay was because their GP's surgery was always busy in the mornings and made their calls in the afternoon.

She took the cordless phone outside with her. And when she was halfway through pulling up a particularly stubborn nettle, the phone rang. She dropped the nettle and grabbed the phone, but too late—the answering-machine had already clicked in and the line had gone dead.

With shaking hands, she punched in 1471 to hear the last number dialled.

'You were called at ten forty-five. The caller withheld their number.'

She could have wept in frustration. She knew it was hospital policy never to leave messages on answering-machines. Why hadn't she checked that hers was switched off? And had it been the hospital, or had it been some cold-calling financial services company, wanting to sell her an insurance policy? Or maybe—please, God, no—maybe her GP's surgery?

She couldn't wait for whoever it was to ring back. And she dared not ring the GP's surgery. She tore her gloves off, went indoors and found the bit of paper the obstetrician had given her. When she rang the number, it was engaged. She cut the connection and tried again. Still engaged. No. They *had* to be there. They had to be. She pressed the redial button and finally the line rang. Four rings. Five. Six.

'Hello, Dr Ashby's secretary speaking.'

'Hello. It's Jennifer Jacobs. Did you…?' Her voice cracked. 'Did you just try to ring me?'

Her heart was beating so loudly she was sure the secretary could hear it. And it was going way, way too fast. This wasn't like an exam result, where you usually knew in your heart whether you'd done enough work to pass or not. This was something outside her control. Please, please, let everything be all right, she begged silently. Please. Please, don't let there be anything wrong with my baby.

'Yes, I did. I'm sorry, it's hospital policy not to leave messages on answering-machines.'

Somehow Jennifer kept her composure. 'Can you tell me the results, please?' The obstetrician had said the hospital would ring if everything was all right. This was the hospital, therefore everything must be all right. But what if?

What if they'd changed the rules since Jennifer's amnio? *What if?*

'I'm delighted to tell you that everything's fine, Mrs Jacobs. The amnio showed no anomalies.'

'Thank you,' Jennifer croaked, hung up and sobbed her eyes out. 'You're fine,' she told her baby, caressing her abdomen. 'Oh, my baby. You're fine.' She offered up a silent prayer of thanks.

Ramón. She ought to tell him. And maybe if the room where he was having his meeting wasn't anywhere near the wards, he might have left his phone switched on.

She picked up the phone again, but her hands were shaking so much that she misdialled. Three times. And then at last she heard his phone ring. Once, twice.

'Ramón Martínez.'

'Ramón? It's…' She couldn't get the words out. Tears were streaming down her face, choking her.

'*Cariña*, stay where you are. I'm coming home.' There was a click and the line went dead.

When she tried to redial, a voice informed her, 'The mobile number you are calling is switched off.'

Please. Keep him safe, she begged silently. Don't let anything bad happen.

Ten minutes later, she heard a car screech to a halt outside. Ramón came running into the house, leaving the front door wide open, and enveloped her in his arms. 'Oh, Jennifer.' He held her tightly. 'It's OK. I will love our baby, no matter what. We both will. We'll be a family together.'

'Ramón, I—'

'Shh. *Tranquilo*,' he said softly. 'I'm here.'

'Ramón, it's all right,' she mumbled against his chest.

'I know.' He stroked her hair. Then paused. 'What do you mean?'

She pulled back far enough to look into his face. 'I was trying to tell you. The results. Everything's all right.'

'But…you were crying. When you rang me, you were incoherent.'

Tears welled in her eyes. 'I still am.'

'I thought…' He swallowed hard. 'I thought it was bad news.'

'I tried to ring you back but you'd switched your mobile off.'

'And I broke every speed limit on the way back.'

'I'm sorry.'

'I'm not.'

'What?' Dread clutched at her stomach. Now he knew everything was all right, did that mean he was going to leave again?

He grinned broadly, picked her up and spun her round. 'We're having a baby, Jennifer. And everything is all right.' He whooped. 'We can tell the world.'

'Ramón—'

'And now we can plan the wedding.'

'Wedding?'

'*Our* wedding,' he emphasised.

'But…you're not going to marry me.'

'Oh, yes, I am.'

'You're just…you're just overreacting because the baby is OK.' And because he thought it was his duty.

'No. You're just hormonal,' he informed her with a grin. 'You're moody and irrational—but it's not your fault, so I won't hold it against you. It's a mixture of progesterone and oestrogen making you feel like this.'

'But—'

'Jennifer, I have no intention of being a weekend father. I don't want to pick our child up on Saturday, go to the park or the zoo or what have you, feed him on indifferent hamburgers and hand over all my responsibilities at the end of the day. I want to be there for all of it. I want to change nappies, do baths, read bedtime stories. I want to be there for the first smile, the first tooth, the first word, the first step—all of it.'

He wasn't smiling. His eyes were so dark and intense and fierce it frightened her. 'You're going to take my baby away from me?' she croaked.

He rolled his eyes. 'Don't be stupid. Of course I'm not going to take our baby away from you. I'm going to be a hands-on father. And husband. And lover.'

CHAPTER FOURTEEN

JENNIFER stared at him, not quite sure she'd heard that last bit correctly. He'd said it in a sensual whisper. *And lover.*

A shudder rippled through her. 'Ramón?'

'Stay put. I'll be back in thirty seconds.' He raced out to the car, then returned with his briefcase. This time he closed the door behind him. He fished in the briefcase for an envelope, extracted a sheet of paper and handed it to her. 'Read it.'

It was a letter confirming his appointment at Brad's. A consultant's position with research duties.

'But...?'

'Look at the date, *cariña.*'

It was dated a week before he'd returned to England.

'I don't understand.'

'Then I'll explain.' He drew her over to the sofa, sat down and pulled her onto his lap. 'I was unhappy in Spain. Very unhappy. Yes, I had my job at the hospital, but it wasn't enough for me any more. I wanted to be here, with you. So the day I got back to Spain, I went to my director, told him I needed to leave there and then for personal reasons and resigned. And I negotiated a new post here at Brad's.'

'But...you and I...'

'Were maybe a little *loco.*' He stroked her hair. 'You thought I was a liar, and I was furious that you could ever believe that of me. We were both angry with each other. But what use is pride if it keeps me away from the woman I love?'

'You love me?'

176

'Haven't I told you so enough times?' He sighed. 'I've already told you that you're the only woman I'm going to marry.' He looked into her eyes. 'The day you told me "I love you" in Spanish, I said something to you. Something maybe I should have said in English. Except I was too scared that I was taking things too fast for you. Maybe I was. I don't know.'

She couldn't speak, her mouth was too dry.

'*Eres toda para mí. Quiero estar contigo para siempre.* You are everything to me,' he translated in a whisper. 'I want to be with you for ever. And that, *mi amor*, is why I am here now. Because my home is where you are,' he said simply.

'You'd be happy to live here?'

'If this is where you want to live, yes.' He shrugged. 'Maybe we will need the house extended in time. Or move to a bigger house—one we choose together—when we have more *niños*.'

When, he'd said. Not if. He wanted to make more babies with her. Have a family with her.

She looked at the letter again. Then she noticed the name at the top. It wasn't addressed to Dr Martínez—it was addressed to Don Martínez.

'What's this?' she asked.

'Ah.' He winced.

'What else aren't you telling me, Ramón?' If he wasn't going to be honest with her, they had no future. Ever. 'Just tell me the truth. All of it.'

'All right. Sofía had a title, which was why her parents weren't keen for her to marry Miguel. She's Señora now, rather than Condessa. And she likes it that way.'

'But if she'd married you, she would still have been Condessa?' Jennifer guessed.

'Mmm-hmm.' Ramón looked embarrassed.

'Then I can't marry you.'

He frowned. 'Why not?'

'Because your family won't accept me.'

He smiled. 'My family is not Sofía's. Of course they will accept you. If you're worrying about Arabela, don't. She's a snob but...' He shrugged. 'She'll get used to it.'

Jennifer had a very nasty thought. 'So Arabela isn't Señora either?'

Ramón burst out laughing. 'No. And she's very prissy about her title.'

'Oh, lord.' Jennifer closed her eyes.

'What is it, *querida*?'

'I...um...when Arabela told me about Sofía, I told her she could find her own way out. And I called her Señora Molinero. I... She'd just introduced herself as Arabela Molinero.'

Still laughing, Ramón rubbed the tip of his nose against hers. 'You weren't to know. Don't worry about it.' His eyes danced with amusement. 'Though I wish I could have seen her face.'

'I thought she just...well, despised me for having no morals,' Jennifer said miserably.

'No, she doesn't despise you at all. Actually, we've spoken about you since she learned the truth about Sofía. She says you have spirit. And that's my sister's way of saying that she will grow to like you.' He stroked her hair. 'My mother will adore you and Pablo will welcome you with open arms. But that's not important.'

She frowned. 'Of course it's important.'

'No. The important thing is us. I want you, Jennifer.'

She exhaled sharply. 'Yeah, right.'

He raised one eyebrow. 'Explain.'

She flushed. 'We've been sharing a bed for over two weeks. You haven't even touched me.'

'No.' An odd smile lit his face. 'I didn't think you wanted me to. You made it pretty clear you wanted me at arm's length, so I tried to respect your wishes. Though it gave me a lot of difficult moments. I only managed half a night on the sofa before I begged you to allow me back in your bed, remember.'

'But…' She flushed. 'You didn't react to me. Physically, I mean.'

'Exactly.' He regarded her seriously. 'Do you have any idea how difficult that was? I had to have a lot of cold showers. And whenever I lay next to you, in my head I went through every single bone of the skeleton, from the skull to the phalanges. And every muscle from the sterno-cleidomastoid to the calcaneal tendon—and your gluteus maximus gave me a very bad moment.' He pulled her closer. 'And then I worked my way through the central nervous system and peripheral nervous system. And then every childhood rash I could think of, together with its possible complications, to stop myself thinking about what I really wanted to do to you.' His voice grew deeper, took on that melted-chocolate quality that had turned her knees to jelly the first time she'd met him. 'Jennifer.' He leaned forward, gently touched his mouth to hers. Nibbled at her lower lip. Brushed his tonguetip against her lips, pleading for her to open her mouth and kiss him properly.

What could she do but kiss him back? And then his control snapped completely and her shirt was on the floor, followed swiftly by her bra, and he was stroking and kissing and tasting every centimetre of skin he'd uncovered.

When he stopped, they were both shaking. And then she realised the curtains were open.

'Ramón! Anyone could see in!' she squeaked.

'Now you know how I feel about you,' he drawled, but he retrieved her shirt and covered her, then closed the curtains. 'I want you, Jennifer. You make me *loco*—you make me crazy with love. But I didn't want to push you, do something I didn't think you were ready for.'

'I didn't think you wanted me.'

'Oh, I did,' he told her, his voice hoarse with sincerity. 'I do. Believe me, I want you. In fact... I think, Jennifer, we need a *siesta*. Right now. So I can prove it.' Without giving her a chance to protest, he scooped her into his arms and carried her up the stairs. Kicked the bedroom door closed behind them. And then undressed her slowly, lingeringly, reacquainting himself with the texture and scent of her skin. Learning how her body had bloomed in pregnancy, how her abdomen was rounded and her breasts were fuller and reacted very gratifyingly to his attentions.

As he pressed a kiss to her belly there was a distinct kick, and Jennifer laughed. 'Jealous.'

'Tough, *niño*. You will need to learn to share your *madre* with me. Your beautiful, gorgeous *madre*. The love of my whole life.'

He made love to her slowly, tenderly. And when she'd climaxed, sobbing his name, he gathered her into his arms.

'So are you going to put me out of my misery and marry me?'

'Was that meant to be a proposal?'

A muscle worked in his jaw. 'Don't tease me now, Jennifer.'

'I'm not. But all you've done so far is inform me that you were going to marry me. You haven't actually *asked* me,' she pointed out.

He sighed heavily. 'That's splitting hairs.'

'That's telling me what to do.'

'And you had enough of that from Andrew.' He stroked her face. 'Spanish men are overbearing. It's genetic. But it will be your job as my wife to tell me when to stop. Because our marriage will be an ''us'', not a ''me''.' He paused. 'If I can persuade you to marry me, that is.'

'Ramón—'

'I know it's meant to be done in moonlight, with me on

one knee and offering you a rose and a glass of champagne and a ring. But I can't wait for moonlight. Don't move.'

'What?'

But he was already striding out of the bedroom. Completely naked. Did the man have no shame? she wondered.

But, then again, a body like that really shouldn't be covered up. Satiated by his love-making, she smiled to herself and settled back against the pillows.

Ramón returned a couple of minutes later with his hands behind his back. 'Imagine the moon,' he commanded.

'Imagine the moon?'

'In your back garden. I did consider carrying you out there...' His eyes travelled down her body, where she hadn't bothered pulling the duvet back over her. 'No. Trust me. You won't be leaving this bed for the rest of today.' He shook his head, as if trying to concentrate. 'Now.' He dropped to one knee and brought one hand from behind his back. 'One glass of water.'

'What happened to the champagne?'

'You're pregnant. It's on hold.' He gave her a smile that heated her blood and placed the glass of water on her bedside table before putting his hand behind his back again and giving her a deep red rose. 'One rose.'

She recognised it as one of her favourites from her garden. Except she knew there weren't any indoors as she hadn't cut any recently. 'Are you telling me you went out into the garden...like that?' she asked faintly.

'Your garden isn't overlooked,' he reminded her with a grin. 'I'm afraid I didn't have the patience to wait and put some clothes on. One drink, one rose, one imaginary moon. Now, Jennifer—*te amo con todo mi corazón. ¿Quieres casarte conmigo?*' Then he translated, his voice low and intensely passionate. 'I love you with all my heart. Will you marry me?'

'I…'

'The word you're looking for is "yes",' he told her.

'And if I say no?'

'I'll ask you on the hour, every hour, until you agree. And I mean *every* hour—I'll set the alarm clock.' He handed her a piece of paper. 'Put me out of my misery, *querida*. Will you marry me? Please?'

Jennifer unfolded the piece of paper and stared at it. 'What's this?'

'What do you think it is?' Typical Ramón, answering a question with a question. 'It's an IOU. For your ring.'

She frowned. 'I'm not with you.'

'I haven't bought you a ring yet. I didn't want to force my choice on you or tell you what to have—I want to buy it with you. So it's an IOU.' He wasn't smiling. To her surprise, he was actually looking anxious. And yet he was always so confident, so sure of himself…

'I love you. From the moment I first saw you, I wanted to be with you. I know you've had your doubts about me, but I can promise you now, I'll never hurt you intentionally, never betray you with another woman, never keep secrets from you, never tell you what to do. Well, except when it's for your own good,' he amended with a grin. 'Any sign of swelling in your ankles and I'll be straight on the phone to Jill the midwife,' he said. 'I don't care where we get married—in a register office, in a church, in the middle of the hospital, in a field. Anywhere. As long as you'll marry me and be my love for the rest of our lives.'

His eyes were amber with a mixture of sincerity and passion, and there was only one thing she could say. 'Yes.'

EPILOGUE

FIVE months later, Jennifer was tucked up in a hospital bed, with Ramón sitting on the bed beside her and their sleeping baby held in her arms.

'I can't believe we made him. He's so perfect,' she said, gazing at her son in wonder. 'And he's really ours.'

'He's really ours,' Ramón echoed, his voice mirroring her wonder.

'Such tiny little fingers.'

'His hands are huge,' Ramón corrected. 'He will be tall.'

'And handsome.' She gave him a sidelong glance. 'Like his father.'

'He has your chin. So he's going to be stubborn and difficult,' Ramón mused.

Jennifer gave her husband an old-fashioned look. 'Right. So José wouldn't have inherited any stubbornness from you, then?'

'Maybe a little,' Ramón said with a grin.

'He has your eyes,' she said. And then a wave of sadness hit her. Maybe José looked like Ramón as a baby. She had no way of knowing what she'd looked like as a baby. No photographs, no one who could tell her and reminisce about her own babyhood.

'Hey. *No pasa nada.*' Ramón, as if he guessed her thoughts, leaned over to kiss her gently. 'I wish your parents could be here to see their grandson, too, but it is not to be. I'm sure they would be proud of you both, as proud as I am.' He smiled. 'And my mother will be enough for both sets of grandparents, believe me.'

Jennifer nodded wryly. Ramón's mother was a female

183

version of her son. Imperious, proud, but with a generous heart—and she'd taken to Jennifer immediately, declaring that anyone who could make her son smile like that would always be welcome in her home. 'You really ought to call her and tell her the news.'

'I will, in a little while. I'll send her a picture message on my mobile so she can see her new grandson. But for now I want to be with you and our son. *Nuestro hijo.*' He held them both close. 'Our family. A family of which you will always be the centre.'

No longer on the sidelines, looking on. Part of a real family. '*Te quiero*, Ramón,' she said.

'And I love you too, *mi esposa. Siempre.* For ever.'

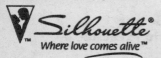

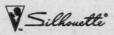

SPECIAL EDITION™

Discover why readers love Sherryl Woods!

THE ROSE COTTAGE SISTERS

Love and laughter surprise them at their childhood haven.

For the Love of Pete
by

SHERRYL WOODS

Jo D'Angelo's sisters knew what she needed—a retreat to Rose Cottage to grieve her broken engagement. And their plan was working—until Jo came face-to-face with the first man ever to break her heart, Pete Catlett, who had ended their idyllic summer love affair when he got another girl pregnant. Pete vowed to gain Jo's forgiveness for his betrayal…and perhaps win her back in the process.

**Silhouette Special Edition #1687
On sale June 2005!**

Where love comes alive™

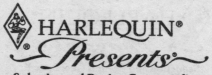

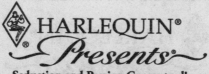

Introducing a brand-new trilogy by

Sharon Kendrick

**Passion, power and privilege—the dynasty
continues with these handsome princes...**

THE
ROYAL HOUSE
OF
CACCIATORE

Welcome to Mardivino—a beautiful and
wealthy Mediterranean island principality,
with a prestigious and glamorous royal family.
There are three Cacciatore princes—Nicolo,
Guido and the eldest, the heir, Gianferro.

This month (May 2005) you can meet Nico in
THE MEDITERRANEAN
PRINCE'S PASSION #2466

Next month (June 2005) read Guido's story in
THE PRINCE'S LOVE-CHILD #2472

Coming in July: Gianferro's story in
THE FUTURE KING'S BRIDE #2478

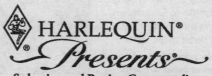

HARLEQUIN®
Presents

Seduction and Passion Guaranteed!

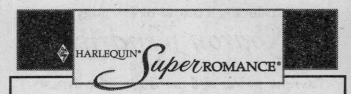

HARLEQUIN *Super*ROMANCE®

Stranger in Town
by
brenda novak

(Superromance #1278)

**Read the latest installment in Brenda Novak's
series about the people of Dundee, Idaho:
STRANGER IN TOWN.**

Gabe Holbrook isn't really
a stranger, but he might as
well be. After the accident—
caused by Hannah Russell—
he's been a wheelchair-bound
recluse. Now Hannah's in his
life again…and she's trying to
force him to live again.

Critically acclaimed novelist
Brenda Novak brings you
another memorable and
emotionally engaging story.
Come home to Dundee—
or come and visit, if you
haven't been there before!

*Available in June 2005 wherever
Harlequin books are sold.*